YOU ARE HERE

JD TURNER

Disclaimer: This book is an uncorrected proof and any errors will be corrected before its official release.

For more information, please visit jdturnerauthor.com.

Copyright © 2023 J.D. Turner

All rights reserved. No part of this book may be reproduced or used in any manner without written permission of the copyright owner except for the use of quotations in a book review.

This book is a work of fiction. References to real people, organisations, events, establishments, or locales are intended only to provide a sense of authenticity, and are used fictitiously. All other characters, and all dialogue and incidents, are drawn from the author's troubled imagination and are not to be construed as real.

ISBN: 979835160728

For Warren

NOVEMBER 2020

I want to take a moment to thank you for your interest in this book. You should know from the onset that what you're about to read isn't about me, but for context, people know me simply as JD, and I've been a writer for a literary magazine called *Pen&Pad* for over ten years. It's likely you've not heard of me, but that's okay because this story isn't about me. It's about a person I'll be referring to as Warren, whose real name I won't reveal out of respect for his privacy.

I first met Warren four years ago. He was just getting started as a writer, but, unlike the other aspiring writers I've met, he didn't come across as particularly ambitious. He even seemed to despise the profession more often than not. Despite this unusual conflict, I took an immediate interest in his work and became fascinated as time passed. He focused on flash fiction and short stories, managing to create exciting concepts within a consumable number of pages—sometimes even just one page. That's what intrigued me the most at first: he didn't indulge himself and always approached writing with minimalist intent. What propelled my intrigue was how these stories provided a personal insight into Warren's mind, which changed how I perceived my own writing and how I looked at the work of others in all forms of art.

It was all so promising at the time, but it started to go wrong when Warren's stories became darker in tone and more sporadic in production. He allowed his ideas to consume him until he eventually stopped writing altogether. To this day, I still don't know why he quit. Well, I have my theories, but he's never given me an explanation. Not a direct one, at least.

It's been almost two years since Warren's last story and even longer since he last replied to one of my emails. I've thought about looking for any mutual connections I might have with him, but I wouldn't even know where to start. I should've expected something like this because Warren's struggles began to reflect in his stories, which I'll go into more detail about soon, but I always believed he'd find a way through and succeed.

I've gathered all of the stories he ever made available to me with the hope of finding some answers. I know there's something I'm missing—something I overlooked or misinterpreted. I'm also hoping you'll enjoy reading them as much as I do, and with that kind of reassurance, maybe Warren will want to start writing again.

Now that you know the end of the story, we can go back to the start so we can try to understand it.

FEBRUARY 2017

It all started at an annual writing festival in London. These events are often tedious when you've been to so many, but there's always plenty of music and food to break up the slower moments reserved for education. I attend these events only to report on them, and if they don't turn out that interesting, I usually find inspiration for an article about something else. It's all a bit hopelessly optimistic, but I enjoy myself either way.

Various special guests were booked to speak in the afternoon. They weren't the most famous of names, but they were promising at the time. After the buffet was raided, everyone crammed into the hall and sat down in front of the stage. The speakers themselves weren't very interesting. In fact, they were so uninteresting that, even with all the notes I took on the speeches, I could give you more details about the food I was eating at the time. It was looking pretty bleak, but then came the Q and A session at the end.

One final question was to be taken, and the microphone was passed to a guy in his mid-twenties who had been eagerly waving his hand. He drew my attention even before he spoke because he was wearing sunglasses, which might not strike you as odd until you consider that we were indoors on an overcast day in February. You'd assume he was just shy, but then why would he volunteer to get up in front of a large crowd to question a complete stranger?

Before I could ponder it further, he tapped the top of the microphone, and in a controlled tone that wasn't rattled by nerves, he said, 'Do you think your thoughts are your own?'

This was Warren.

There were a few laughs among the crowd. I thought it was a wind-up, but Warren maintained composure and awaited a response. I can't remember if he directed the question at a specific speaker, but none of them responded. There was just awkward silence. I've had years to think about the possible answers now, but I didn't think much of it at the time because I had no way of knowing its significance. It wasn't the best question to end on, being that it went unanswered, but the audience didn't complain and looked almost relieved that it was over. I suppose they were more eager to queue up for an autograph.

The special guests took their leave after complaining about hand cramps, and various workshops were held around the venue for the remainder of the event. I didn't have a particular schedule for the day, so I hovered in and out of rooms, hoping to find something worthwhile for the magazine. It was just after a marketing workshop that I ran into Warren. Actually, I spotted him from a distance and called for his attention. I must have looked like a confused fan. I couldn't help but immediately bring up his question from the Q and A. I anticipated a revelation upon hearing his explanation, but he turned it back on me and asked if I had my own answer. I didn't, of course. He knew I didn't. I tried to get a clue out of him, but he was adamant that I think about it before he discussed it. I was slightly annoyed, so I changed tactics and started with some probing questions.

Warren was very deflective at first, as though he was the head chef and I was trying to steal his secret ingredient to sell to a competing restaurant, but the more we talked, the more eager he was to share. I can't recall the discussion word for word because it happened years ago, so excuse the lack of dialogue. I was surprised to learn that he wasn't much of a reader. He was an independent animator, but, having completed hundreds of commissions since graduating, he'd worked himself to exhaustion and lost his passion for animation. He couldn't let it go completely because it was his main source of income, so he found an escape in the narrative side of his trade, which quickly became far more exciting than animation ever was for him.

He'd only been writing for a few months at that point. He'd written short stories, poems, thought pieces and scripts inside one notebook that he always kept with him. The notebook looked old and worn, but you could tell it was by design and not genuinely vintage. It was bound by hand using distressed leather and filled with yellowed paper. He said he picked it up at a flea market while travelling Europe. The woman who sold it to him never planned to sell it due to its sentimental value. She had always wanted to fill the pages herself, but her arthritis was so severe that she couldn't write by hand for more than a few seconds at a time. So, with the promise that the pages would be filled, she gave it to Warren for nothing. No haggling needed. It was a great deal if you don't consider the overpriced souvenir mug and snow globe he'd already purchased from her.

After I told Warren a bit about myself, I talked him into sharing one of his short stories with me. Before we go any further, I want you to read that story so we can start to understand the person behind it. This is only to give you a sense of Warren's early style, so don't worry if it confuses you as it did me; however, to help a little, I've inserted numbers before each section so you can keep track of which level you're on.

The Perfect Twist

1

'Did you hear what I said?'

Tommy looked at Brooks, his agent, with a blank expression. 'You didn't say anything.'

'Right you are,' Brooks replied. 'Just making sure you're listening before I tell you what I'm about to tell you.'

'Tell me then,' Tommy insisted.

'I am telling you, this is part of it, and you're interrupting.'

Tommy stared in silence for a moment. Neither of them could find a queue to speak.

'Don't ignore me,' Brooks said.

'I'm not ignoring you. I'm listening.'

'Don't be funny with me, Tommy.'

'I'm not trying to be funny. I'd come here with a comedy manuscript if that was my goal.'

'You know full well I don't deal with comedy,' Brooks said, slapping the desk. 'But that brings me back to that thing I wanted to tell you.'

'Which is?'

'I have an idea,' Brooks proudly announced.

Tommy leaned forward. 'Go on.'

'What if... you had an idea?'

Tommy sat back. 'What?'

'Not just any idea, a great idea.' Brooks slapped the desk again, this time with both hands, and then he folded his arms with a satisfied smile.

'That's it? Your idea is for me to have an idea?' Tommy puzzled.

'No, no. You misunderstand me, Tommy. I want you to have a moment of genius, or as close as someone like you can get to one. I want something with a twist. A big twist!'

Tommy scratched his chin stubble. 'So... you're not requesting another specific premise? Not even a genre? It was post-apocalyptic agriculture last week, and now you just want a story with a twist?'

'The twist is the premise,' Brooks replied, touching the end of his nose. 'See, that's a little twist within itself. And Jerry has already given me a heart-wrenching manuscript on post-apocalyptic agriculture. You need to keep up.'

'Fine. How long do I have?'

Brooks squinted, lifted his chin, and then spun three hundred and sixty degrees in his chair. 'You've already done it, haven't you?'

'Whatever do you mean?' Tommy replied with a cheeky smile. 'You saw the glint in my eye, didn't you?'

'What glint?' Brooks asked, sticking his head forward.

'You got me! I have indeed done it. How did you guess?'

The edges of Brooks' mouth started to twitch as he held eye contact. He furrowed his brow and tried to hold it, but it collapsed under the weight of his grin and forced a laugh from his lungs. 'In the nature of a twist, what's more twisty than that?'

'You've got a point there.' Tommy removed a shabby notebook from the bag between his feet and handed it to Brooks.

'Not even a printed and bound manuscript? You're slacking, Tommy.'

'I'm not slacking. In fact, I'm lacking in slack, so why don't you cut me some?'

'Come again?'

'Look, I'm here delivering a manuscript within a minute of

THE PERFECT TWIST

your request. That's surely a record.'

'Fair point, Tommy.' Brooks opened the notebook and started reading below the title: The Perfect Twist.

2

I had done it. I had written the perfect twist. My agent had been requesting it for quite some time now, but thanks to his patience, and my perseverance, it was finished and ready for the eyes of my peers.

'Sit down then,' my agent, Brooks, said.

'I am sitting down,' I replied to him, although it felt like my mind hadn't done the same.

'I know. I was just making sure you were listening so you hear what I want you to hear.'

'The floor is all yours,' I said with an affirming nod.

'This office is rented, so it technically isn't all mine, but I digress. I have something of the utmost importance to tell you.'

'As I said, I'm listening.'

'Not quite what you said, was it, Tommy boy.'

'Don't be pedantic now.'

'I don't deal in pedantism—you know that. Anyway, I have a concept.'

I leaned forward, expecting something life-changing.

'You should come up with a concept.'

I sat back. Even I could somehow see the disappointment on my face. 'Your concept is for me to come up with a concept?' I asked.

'Not just any concept, a concept with a twist.'

'Is there a particular genre or theme? Last week it was religious sciences.'

'Ah, here's the kicker. The concept is the twist.' Brooks sat back, placed his hands confidently behind his head, and put his feet on his desk. 'Oh, and I admit I may have crossed the line with the genre of religious sciences. Jerry came up with this daft story called "Darwin's Theory of God's Relativity", and I quickly realised how ridiculous the whole idea was.'

'Jerry's a moron, but I'm not sure what you're asking of me.'

'It's simple, Tommy. I want a story about a twist that slowly unravels but is always tangled. Do you think you can handle that?'

Of course I can handle it, I thought to myself. I had handled it. I turned away to hide the glint in my eye.

'I saw that glint in your eye,' Brooks said.

'What are you talking about?' I replied, barely holding back a smile.

'It's by my own deduction that I have deduced that you've already got something for me along the lines of my request.'

I couldn't hold back the smile any longer, and it spread across my cheeks. 'I don't know what kind of equation would bring you to that conclusion, but it's spot on.' I reached into my bag and removed a bound manuscript with a laminated title page.

'Wow, look at that. I'm impressed.'

'What did you expect?' I replied, handing over the manuscript. 'A rough draft inside the back end of a notebook? Please.'

Brooks opened the manuscript with his signature greasy smile plastered across his face.

1

Brooks closed the notebook and set it down softly.
'Tommy,' he said, 'this seems a lot like the interaction we had

THE PERFECT TWIST

just a moment ago.'

'You're quite right, Brooks,' Tommy swiftly countered. 'In fact, it was the inspiration for my narrative and its characters.'

'I mean, you've made some interesting choices. You've written me a little... arrogant.'

'This is just a character—it isn't actually you. That within itself is an arrogant thing to assume.'

Brooks nudged his seat back to get a better position under the air conditioning. 'I see your point, but it does read like a parody of me. Surely you can agree.'

'Now Brooks, I know you're testing me here because you don't deal in parody. You would've requested a parody premise if that was the case.'

Brooks picked up the notebook and scanned the text. 'Well, what about this insult to Jerry?'

'Which one did I put?'

'That he's a moron. I thought you got along with him?'

'We do get along. It's just a bit of joshing.'

'And the religious sciences? It feels like you're mocking me. On top of that, you've even written yourself delivering a bound manuscript while I'm sat here with a tattered notebook. There's a shopping list on the opposite page.'

Tommy exhaled. 'Need I remind you that this is fiction? I'm not writing an autobiography here.'

'That's... logic I can't argue with.'

'Out of curiosity, what colour ink is the shopping list written in?'

Brooks paused to inspect the ink, holding it up to the light to get an accurate evaluation. 'Blue, I believe.'

'Oh, no bother, that's from last week.'

'That's... good to know. Right. More importantly, where's the perfect twist?'

'I can't tell you that. It'll spoil it.'

'But I've read it. What's there to spoil? Am I missing something here?'

Tommy took the notebook and turned the page. 'The story picks up from here.'

'Ah. With there being a shopping list on the very next page, you can see how that would bring me to assume it was the end, right?'

'Yes, I can see that.'

'Well, I guess that makes it okay then,' Brooks replied, massaging his forehead with his fingertips. 'So this picks up where I—'

'Where Brooks,' Tommy corrects. 'It's not really you.'

'Yes, where "fictional" Brooks opens the manuscript with his'—Brooks eyed Tommy over the top of the notebook—'greasy smile.'

'That's correct. So this is what's written in the bound manuscript that *not you* is now reading.'

'Why greasy?'

'That's just characterisation.'

'Of course it is,' Brooks muttered, looking back at the page.

3

I looked at my client, Tommy, over the top of the notebook and said, 'This seems awful familiar.'

'Of course it does,' Tommy replied. 'It's based on the interaction we just had and what I assume to be the interaction that follows.'

'Yes, it's impressive. But I'm not sure about some of the deviations from reality.'

'It's fiction, Brooks. You need to remember that.'

I sighed and repositioned myself to be slightly under the air conditioning. Tommy was right, and suddenly there was something about the attention to detail that made me feel... honoured.

'Don't hold out on me now,' Tommy said. 'What do you think?'

'It reads like a tribute. You've used some well-realised nuances about me and have sown them seamlessly among the fabric of the story. And I love the jibe at Jerry. Great stuff.'

'I know you don't like to deal with tributes,' Tommy began with a cheeky grin, 'but I hope to make this the exception. And I knew you'd enjoy the part where we conclude that Jerry is, in fact, a moron.'

'He really is, isn't he. One time he came to me with an idea for a book about a film that shows a film crew making a film on how to make a film that's adapted from a book. Absolutely ludicrous. That "Darwin's Theory of God's Relativity" sounds exactly like the sort of thing he would come up with.'

I watched as Tommy chuckled to himself for a moment. I'm quite the funny guy when I want to be, and that's how I maintain a healthy working relationship with so many of my writers. I see them as friends more than anything. It also enables me to demand higher fees than standard rates, but we don't talk about that often.

'I must say I adore this notebook,' I said over Tommy's charming laugh. 'I'm used to pristine final drafts printed on fine paper, roughly seventy-four grams and no less than ninety-four per cent brightness, which all sounds great on paper, pun intended, but I much prefer this notebook. It gives it a personal touch.'

'That was my intention,' Tommy replied. 'I hope the print copies could reflect that on the cover.'

'I'm sure we could sort something out. Now, about that twist.'

2

Brooks looked at me over the top of the pristine manuscript, his greasy smile now dry.

'What do you think?' I asked.

'I'm getting a sense of déjà vu,' Brooks replied.

'Aha, you're almost correct. That sense is of pre-déjà vu, which you'll understand later.'

'So my... I mean, Brooks' reaction to what's written in Tommy's notebook is an interpretation of my reaction to your manuscript.'

'Thereabouts,' I said, having somewhat deciphered his riddle of my twist.

'So what was written in the notebook?'

'Depends which notebook?'

'Isn't there just the one?' Brooks said, his head tilting backwards as though all of his confusion had forced too much blood to rush into his brain.

I cleared my throat. 'Putting it simply, the characters inside the notebook that's inside the manuscript are reacting to the same notebook that's inside this manuscript. It includes everything we've said and whatever we're going to say.'

'We're writing it now?'

'In a way, yes.'

'This is... brilliant. That moron Jerry could never have come up with something like this. And I like the reference in this manuscript of Jerry being a moron, which must have been referenced in the notebook, which would have originally come from the manuscript that is essentially the same as this manuscript. So what about this other notebook?'

I held his stare and said, 'It's the same notebook.'

1

Brooks lowered the notebook. 'Are they referring to this notebook?'

Tommy sighed and said, 'Yes and no.'

'Is this the same notebook as in the manuscript?'

'I didn't know there would be a Q and A.'

Brooks closed his eyes and pinched the bridge of his nose. 'The notebook inside their manuscript is the same notebook as the one in front of me? Yes or no?'

'Putting it like that, no. How on earth could it be the same? I would've just copied and pasted this otherwise and put it as the manuscript that's inside the notebook.'

Brooks' eyes went wide.

'Déjà vu?' Tommy asked.

Brooks nodded. 'Are we a manuscript?' he asked.

Tommy cracked a knuckle under his thumb. 'Please just keep reading.'

2

Brooks looked away from my eyes and up to the ceiling like he'd come to a revelation. 'You know what, I get it,' he said, his eyes falling back to mine. 'And I bet you expected me to ask you nonsensical questions.'

'Of course not,' I replied. 'I know you know this isn't a Q and A. You're smarter than that.'

'To be honest with you, Tommy, I know that you know that I know that. I was just baiting a compliment.'

1

Brooks looked up at Tommy with an accusation on the tip of his tongue.

'Don't,' Tommy said, putting up his finger. 'Just don't.'

2

Brooks frowned and said, 'So, with this being the same manuscript that was given to the Brooks that was in the notebook that was given to the Brooks in this manuscript, is this manuscript really printed on seventy-four-gram paper with ninety-four per cent brightness?'

I pondered the difficult question.

I knew very little about paper. 'I think I'll leave that to interpretation. I don't really want to have to explain everything. Besides, you can turn the page and read the rest now.'

'Oh wow, there's another page.'

'Yep, there's a lot more pages.'

'I only have... two.'

'The rest are in the notebook,' I said, tapping my nose.

'Ah, how silly of me, of course they are.' Brooks laughed as he turned the page and continued to read.

3

'The twist?' Tommy replied, looking surprised by my question.

'Well, what is it?' I asked.

'I haven't got to it yet.'

Tommy always had a habit of turning in one piece of his

THE PERFECT TWIST

work at a time. It would've bothered me if not for the high standards he maintained.

'You mean you're not done writing it?' I said.

'It's been written, but it's not yet been read.'

That would be an excellent quote for bookmarks, I thought. I could give them away for free with every paperback. I had no idea what Tommy meant by it, but it inspired the marketing genius deep within me.

'I know exactly what you mean,' I replied.

'I knew you would,' Tommy said with a wink. 'So, do we have a deal?'

'I guess we do.'

We stood up and shook hands with intense eye contact.

2

'So?' Brooks said.

'So what?' I replied.

'Did Brooks' bookmark idea go over well?'

'That's neither written nor would ever be read.'

Brooks chuckled. 'Very clever.'

I doubt he had any idea what was so clever about it, mainly because I had no idea either. I let him laugh himself tired until he sighed and turned his attention back to the manuscript.

'I guess there's no need for further discussion,' he said, standing up. 'You've delivered, and it seems I've already accepted.'

'It seems like you have,' I replied, bursting to my feet.

'Where do we go from here?' he asked as he shook my hand.

I looked him dead in the eye, just so he'd notice the glint once more, and said, 'The next page.'

1

'What next page?' Brooks said, disrupting the sound of his heavy breathing.

'This page,' Tommy replied with confidence.

'I do see what you're going for here, but it's not exactly what I was hoping for. I need something a little more... definitive.'

'It will be.'

'If you want to come back with something else, I'll be happy to read it, but if you need a little help on where to go with this story, there's no shame in getting some advice from Jerry.'

'Jerry. Good old Jerry. Great guy. Better friend.'

'That's a bit passive-aggressive, Tommy. It's the same with how you've written me in this notebook. You exaggerate and portray me as a gullible, arrogant character. Well, characters, technically.'

'Brooks, please don't talk about my characters that way. You wouldn't like it if I insulted your kids, would you?'

Brooks slowly nodded for a good minute and then took a breath and said, 'I'll be in touch.'

Tommy stared.

'Anything else, Tommy?'

'Just waiting for the glint.'

'For goodness sake, what glint are you talking about?'

'There it went,' Tommy replied with a smile.

0

Brooks places the manuscript on the desk and takes a moment to reflect. 'Why did I turn it down?' he finally asks.

THE PERFECT TWIST

'You didn't,' I reply, offering my hand.

'Oh, that's good. That's really good. You've got yourself a deal.'

'Was there any doubt?' I say as our hands meet for a very warm and moist handshake. It lasts a good couple of minutes.

'Was that the twist?' Brooks asks as he slips his hand from mine.

'There was no twist,' I answer with a cheeky wink. 'And that... is the twist.'

Brooks' jaw drops. 'You know, this brilliance is why Tommy will never make it in this industry,' he says as we reach the door.

I look back at Brooks with a wide smile. 'Tommy is a moron.'

'He is a moron. Anyway, I'll be in touch. Take care, Jerry.'

[February 2017]

It can get quite confusing, I know. It took me a couple of reads to grasp what was going on, but you can easily make sense of the narrative if you pay attention to the numbers and the shifts in the point of view. The main takeaway from this story is how we assume to know others and manipulate them to suit our needs. Tommy is never really Tommy, he's interpreted by Jerry the whole time, and that's the same with all the perspectives presented within the layers of the story. However, you have to look beyond the reveal at the end for the actual twist. Jerry made Tommy out to be self-important and arrogant because he wanted to turn Brooks against him for his own gain, so the real twist was that the reader's perception of Tommy was being twisted by Jerry all along. That's how I see it, anyway.

One peculiar detail is how Brooks dictates his client's work. It's obviously not a realistic portrayal of a literary agent, but it gave me the impression that this story was based on a bad experience. It wasn't aggressive in its characterisation, though, and I found it quite funny. Ultimately, I viewed this story as a meta-comedy with an experimental structure, and that's all it needed to be.

I wanted to begin with this story because it gives us a neutral starting point so you can see how Warren's work develops over the years. *The Perfect Twist* is quite relaxed compared to his more recent stories, which might seem hard to believe, but the narrative isn't driven by anything other than its own concept. At this early stage, Warren was only interested in experimenting with unconventional ways of telling a story rather than exploring the kind of ideas that I've come to expect from him.

I asked Warren if I could feature The Perfect Twist in March's edition of *Pen&Pad* with it fully credited to him. He wouldn't receive any money for it, but I thought the exposure would be enticing enough. It would've required approval from the editor, but that was just a formality. I had a strong relationship with the publication and was rarely turned down.

'Nope,' Warren politely said.

I couldn't believe it. Up until that moment, I had asked hundreds of writers if I could feature their work, and not one of them had given me a "nope". I wasn't offended, but I was frustrated. Why on earth would a budding writer turn down an opportunity to get his story seen by thousands? This was yet another question lingering on my mind that I had no possible answer to. I tried to get an explanation from him, but all he'd say was that he didn't think it was right for him at that time. I gave him my email and told him that if he changed his mind or just needed an opinion on his work, I'd be happy to help. In all honesty, I never expected to hear from him again, just like many other writers I've met at similar events. Fortunately, I was wrong, and he got in touch with me just a week later.

The first email Warren sent was headed with the subject "ive". And yes, it takes a while to get used to his offbeat humour. He said he'd taken my advice and started writing digitally; I told him at the conference that it would be easier to edit and organise his work if he used a computer. He was hesitant at first because he wanted more time away from screens, but he conceded that it would make the process less of a headache for him in the long run.

At the bottom of the email, Warren left a link to an online folder he created to share his work with me. The folder was called "rename later". I couldn't tell if this was a placeholder or just another example of his humour, but it hasn't been renamed to this day. Inside this folder was a photocopy of every page in Warren's notebook. They weren't the easiest to decipher due to the handwriting and quality of the scans, but there was no chance of him typing them up because he hated revisiting his work, so it was the best I was going to get. He once told me that progress only comes when you let go of what's holding you back, which has to be done without expecting to get the desired conclusion. Sounds infuriating to me.

I spent a few days going through the folder, but it only provided a glimpse of what Warren could do. He struggled to fully realise his stories—*The Perfect Twist* was the longest he'd written and the only one that had an ending. But all this sporadic writing wasn't for nothing, and I told him he had a backlog of intriguing characters and niche narrative premises that could be utilised. He didn't see it that way, though. He considered it practice and didn't like to recycle anything that hadn't previously worked out for him. The only stories he'd revisit were those intended to be written in parts—stories that benefited from a change in the writer's perspective. I initially thought this would cause inconsistencies, but he used this approach in one of my favourite stories of his, but we'll get to that later.

It took me a couple of days to go through everything made available to me, and then I sent Warren this email:

"I appreciate you sharing your work with me. There's some interesting stuff here, but I'm anticipating a bigger story. Are you working on anything like that at the moment?"

Warren replied back immediately with a resounding "No."

It was a bit blunt, but I accepted he wasn't great at conversation. I told him to keep me updated and left him to it.

APRIL 2017

Contact with Warren faded out through March into April. I wondered if I had offended him when I asked if he was working on something bigger. I didn't mean to suggest that *The Perfect Twist* wasn't substantial enough, but I figured his stories would naturally get longer and denser because that's how most writers progress.

I spoke to a few friends who also wrote for *Pen&Pad,* and they all thought I was lying about Warren. They wouldn't believe an aspiring writer would reject publication, so I had to show them the story to convince them I wasn't making it up. That confirmation only confused them, but it was helpful to know that I wasn't alone in my musings. I knew I had to convey that sense of belonging to Warren, no matter how long it would take.

I checked to make sure I still had access to *rename later* and found a new story that had been there for a week. I figured Warren would've let me know about it, but I didn't think too much of it.

A Tale of Two Pronouns

'What's your concern?'

'I think she's hiding something,' he begins. 'I can feel it. She's always avoiding eye contact and snapping at me randomly. She's growing more distant by the day.'

'He's got a secret,' she begins. 'I don't know what it could be, though. He's always watching me, but he never pays attention to the things that matter. It's like he doesn't want to get close anymore.'

'You've not mentioned anything to each other?'

'I think she knows I'm suspicious of her,' he continues. 'I can see it in her face. There's no warmth like there used to be—she's cold from her cheeks to her fingertips. I force a smile when I see her, hoping she smiles back, but she never does.'

'He seems cautious,' she continues. 'I shiver whenever he's near—I can't help it. I get so nervous. And he's always flinching when I touch him. He still smiles, but his eyes don't. It's just a hollow grin.'

'Why don't you say something?'

'I've tried multiple times,' he said, 'but she always changes the subject. She talks about her work and friends—anything to avoid meaningful conversation.'

'How can I?' she says. 'He doesn't even want to talk to me about how my day went. It's cliché, I know, but he always used to ask. Now he rolls his eyes when I bring up anything like that.'

'Do you think it will last between you both?'

'Honestly, no,' he says, covering his eyes. 'I want her to want to stay, but it's like she's halfway out the door already.'

Her eyes tear up. 'I doubt it. I wish it would, but I don't think he'd even chase me if I walked out.'

'What's the one thing you want to say but can't?'

'That I love her.'

'That I love him.'

'And the one thing to hear back?'

'She still loves me.'

'He still loves me.'

* * *

[April 2017]

When I read this for the first time, I wasn't sure what to think. It wasn't bad, but it wasn't what I expected. It's a concept-driven narrative, much like *The Perfect Twist*, but it lacks that characterisation and complexity. However, I realise now that I was overly critical and only focused on what was missing instead of what it offered. After re-reading it as part of this book, without any expectations clouding my mind, I discovered a much bigger story being told here than I first thought.

The plot is leveraged by a lack of communication, and to convey a sense of disconnect, Warren eliminates all description and narration, using only dialogue to tell the story. It allows the reader to place themselves into the scene as either character while the writer serves as a mediator. And I believe this is the whole point of the story. It's designed to provoke emotion. I can't say for sure what it's supposed to make you feel, but in my case, it makes me feel responsible—even guilty. Most people can relate to having a difficult experience that could've been avoided if more had been said.

This is what I find so fascinating about Warren's stories. They're simplistic in nature but complex through interpretation. Whether he intended ambiguity in his writing, I can't say for sure, but stories inherently inspire thoughts and feelings, and readers have more control over stories than they realise, given the lack of relationship they have with the writers. Still, I do believe it's sometimes beneficial to know the writer more intimately because you see things you wouldn't usually notice, and if there's anything I learned from my experience with Warren, it's that you have to understand the parts before you can comprehend the whole.

I sent Warren my thoughts on *A Tale of Two Pronouns* and asked what inspired him to write it, hoping to get a small insight into his life rather than the story.

The next day, I received a reply that was entirely contained within the subject matter.

It read: "That's not for me to say."

His response made me think this was a little more personal than I anticipated, and it's not uncommon for creators to seek empathy through their work. The use of pronouns might have been less about the concept and more about making it less intimate for his own sake. While it made a lot of sense for him to have found inspiration in a past relationship, I couldn't know for sure. Either way, I figured he could use a distraction, so I invited him to a book reading that a friend of mine was hosting at her local library, celebrating her debut novel. He accepted the invitation but didn't seem very enthusiastic about it.

Warren arrived late to the reading wearing the same sunglasses he'd worn to the conference back in February. I can't say I was surprised. I waited until Sarah finished reading the first chapter of her book, and then I sat down with Warren for a chat in the coffee shop across the road.

'That's the first book reading I've been to,' Warren said, trying not to spill his coffee as he sat down. 'I didn't know what to expect, but I might do this more often.'

'What did you think of Sarah's book?' I asked, picking the tomatoes out of my store-bought sandwich. 'From what she read anyway.'

'Romance isn't really my thing,' he replied.

'You enjoy reading, though?'

'Yes, but that doesn't mean I have to like all genres. You like sandwiches, right?'

'Well, yeah,' I said, looking down at my sandwich and back up at Warren.

'But you clearly don't like tomatoes, so you take them out. You see what I mean?'

'Okay, I get your point there, but what if we talk objectively?'

'I don't know how to answer that,' he said, taking off his sunglasses.

His eyes looked far wearier than I remembered from the little I had glimpsed of them in February. I suppose being an animator does that to you with all the late nights staring at screens.

'I understand if you didn't relate or connect to it,' I replied, 'but it's well written, don't you think?'

'I don't have to relate to a story to enjoy or appreciate it.'

'Sure,' I said, folding my arms, 'but it's more powerful if you do.'

'I don't think we're talking objectively anymore.'

'You don't think your stories are relatable?'

'I didn't say that.'

'I thought *A Tale of Two Pronouns* was extremely relatable —for a selected audience.'

'That says more about you than the story,' he said with a laugh. 'Read it again.'

We went back and forth like this for a while, and Warren concluded that stories can make you feel something or nothing and be entertaining either way. There was no one way about it in his mind, but I wasn't trying to refute any of that. I just wanted him to consider his own audience. I told him his work would suit those looking for a connection through emotion.

'Intent doesn't have to permit an outcome,' Warren said.

This was a problem. If he wanted to be successful, he needed to play to his strengths.

'If you don't establish your intent, you'll just confuse your readers,' I firmly replied.

He stood, put his sunglasses back on, and said, 'Confusion is the first step to a pleasant surprise,' almost like he'd rehearsed it in the mirror that morning.

It was at this point that I started wondering why I was so

eager for him to succeed as an author. I knew plenty of writers with so much talent who could produce a full-length novel within a year, yet I found myself impatiently awaiting short tales from someone I knew nothing about—someone too stubborn for his own good. Maybe it was something to do with helping a writer hone his skills and the satisfaction of acknowledgement that comes with it. Even to this day, I can't explain my reasons. Despite my uncertainty, I was eager for his next story.

MAY 2017

I was doing a lot of thinking throughout the month. I thought a lot about the conversation I had with Warren, but I still couldn't make sense of it. Not only did he not want his story shared, but he also hated the idea of catering to an audience. The audience should've meant everything to him because they would've been the ones reading his stories if he had kept at it. Many young writers miss this point, but they all eventually see the importance of strategy. I just hoped Warren would follow that trend and realise that sometimes you have to think of your stories as a product, but it doesn't mean you have to be less creative. I only wanted him to understand my position so he wouldn't throw away his passion based on misconceptions.

Warren uploaded a new file at the end of the month. This one was titled "Relatable Jeff". I thought it was a satirical wind-up at first, but it was actually the perfect response to our last conversation and the kind of story I was hoping to read.

Relatable Jeff

Jeff lives alone. He has no friends, a boring job, no love life, and a rubbish haircut. Jeff is relatable. His routine is as you'd expect: wake up, go to work, come home, and sleep. He would never admit it out loud, mainly because he has nobody to admit it to and isn't into the habit of talking to himself, but he is very lonely and deeply unhappy. However, Jeff's life is about to change—he just doesn't know it yet.

Like any other day, Jeff wakes up alone in his bed. He looks at the empty space next to him and wonders why his wife isn't beside him. Did she go to work early? Jeff wonders. His mind slips out of its groggy state, and he remembers he doesn't have a wife. He's completely alone, as I've already mentioned, but all that is about to change.

After a quick shower, Jeff dresses for work and heads downstairs for breakfast. What should I have? Jeff questions internally, despite knowing he'd already decided to have toast. He always had toast. Dry toast with a cup of... oh, pardon me, today he's decided to have an omelette. That's most unusual. Never mind, I suppose Jeff can have some leeway in his routine. I'll allow this one little discrepancy.

Jeff stands at a distance as the egg mixture sizzles and spits inside the pan. He'd used far too much oil. He would never care to use such things sparely, and why would he? He only requires enough to serve one throughout the month because, as I have already told you, he is alone. No wife, no kids, no friends, and no living relatives. Jeff believes his misfortune is due to his life being entirely fictional, as though he was simply a tool in a very depressing story. But that would be silly.

Once the omelette is slightly browned on either side, Jeff takes it to the table and uses tomato sauce to decorate it with a smiley face. He does this to remind himself of what it looks like to be happy, but his misery only grows upon seeing just how happy the omelette appears.

The clock ticks above the dining room table. It's only 6:30am. Jeff has plenty of time before work, and he'll need it too. As Jeff begins neatly sectioning the smiling omelette for more efficient consumption, the phone starts ringing. The shock almost knocks Jeff from his seat. He doesn't know what the sound is at first because nobody ever calls him. He realises where the noise is coming from, and an ache hits him in the chest. Who could this possibly be, he ponders. He has no idea his life is about to change for the better.

Jeff approaches the phone and immediately picks... oh, wait, I think he's stuck in thought. He must still be pondering who's calling, but surely he knows he should hurry up and answer it? Right? Jeff? Come on, just pick up—well, for some reason, Jeff decides to wait until the phone stops ringing. Perhaps he prefers the loneliness of silence? Luckily, Jeff is granted another opportunity when the phone starts ringing again, and this time Jeff isn't startled. Jeff is determined to answer it because he knows there's a small chance this will change his life forever.

'Hello?' a kind voice says from the other end of the phone.

Jeff correctly assumes this is a simple case of someone dialling the wrong number, but what he doesn't know is that it will soon become the right number.

'Hello?' the kind voice repeats. 'It's Jenny. Is this Bill?'

For a moment, knowing that this woman has nothing to do with him, Jeff thinks about hanging up, but instead—oh, for God's sake, Jeff! What are you thinking? He hung up. Who just hangs up like that? What's wrong with you? Is it too much

RELATABLE JEFF

to ask you to converse with a random caller? Yeah, go back to your pathetic cheerful omelette. Are you looking forward to another dull day at work? That claustrophobic bus ride?

Bus ride... there's an idea.

Right, new plan. I can fix this, Jeff. We still have time. No, we don't have time, that's it!

Jeff glances up at the clock as he chews the last piece of his omelette, and he turns cold upon seeing the time. He stops chewing, leans forward, and then gulps: it's already ten to eight! But how? He's always careful not to take his time to eat breakfast. He prides himself on great time management skills—it's in bold on his CV. Had he misread the clock earlier on? Had he set his alarm an hour late? He doesn't have time to question reality and accepts that he simply wasn't paying attention. This carelessness was very out of character for him.

He heads to his bedroom and puts on one of his three identical suits. It's a dark grey cotton cocoon of a suit. He puts one on every day with the hope it fits a little less tightly, but it's never to be. He buttons his shirt up to his neck where his collar begins to itch, and he's ready to—oh no, he's forgotten his trousers. Lovely. Jeff realises this at the top of the stairs when he looks down to see his hairy legs. He runs back to his bedroom, jumps into a pair of creased trousers, and wraps a belt around his waist, tightening it to the last hole. The buckle always digs into his stomach when walking, but Jeff is used to it. Why even bother trying to fix it after all this time, he would often conclude.

Jeff leaves the house and runs for the bus. Actually, it's more of a slow jog than a run. He refuses to run for buses because he likes to think they run for him. Fortunately, the bus is running a little late and arrives as soon as he reaches the shelter. The bus, like Jeff, was always on schedule, and Jeff thought it utterly peculiar that they both upset the natural order of things on the very same day. But he doesn't dwell on the thought for too long because he doesn't want to give himself a migraine.

The bus is full of familiar faces. Not that Jeff knows any of them—they were just frequent users of that particular bus. One particular face, however, stands out more than the rest. It's one that belongs to Judy, a girl he works with at the supermarket. What on earth is she taking the bus for, Jeff ponders, knowing she owns a blue Honda Civic. She wouldn't shut up about it when she bought it to replace her electric scooter. She even offered to give Jeff a lift on several occasions, but Jeff didn't want to put her out of her way. He's too mild-mannered for his own good if you ask me.

As Jeff walks towards the back of the bus, Judy makes eye contact and smiles. Jeff smiles back and sits next—oh, for goodness' sake, he's walked straight past her. What on earth is he doing? Oh look, he's realised his favourite spot at the back of the bus is empty. That's it. You're forcing my hand here, Jeff.

A sudden red light prompts the bus driver to slam on the break, throwing Jeff several feet backwards.

The bus driver pokes his head out from his cage. 'Sorry about that, everyone,' he yells. 'These fucking lights,' he added under his breath.

Jeff looks up from the floor and sees Judy looking down at him. He smiles, but only to hide the embarrassment.

'You okay?' she asks.

Jeff nods.

'Maybe you should just sit here with me before the driver decides to throw down his led foot again.'

Judy glances out the window as Jeff climbs into the seat next to her.

'Do you hate buses as much as I do?' she asks, turning back to Jeff.

Jeff looks up and... Jeff? Look up, buddy. Jeff? You little ingrate—he's popped in his earphones and closed his eyes. I forgot about his pathetic little MP3 player. The old-fashioned

RELATABLE JEFF

fool.

Right, I didn't want to resort to this, but I'm left with little choice. Just for your ignorance, we're doing this the extreme way.

The first track of *Ocean Waves Volume Ten* begins, and Jeff allows the sound of water brushing and fizzing across the sand to free his mind from all concern. His body loosens, and he feels himself melting into his seat as a soothing dream teases his mind. A dream in which he's asleep and sees himself sleeping. It seems to go on endlessly, but the dream soon fades into darkness as he's gently eased back into the light.

Jeff opens his eyes to find himself sitting at a long table in a narrow room. He recognises it as the staff canteen that's among the upstairs offices in the supermarket he works at. He's sure he was on the bus not five minutes ago, but he couldn't have been because he isn't, and it would be crazy to think otherwise. Wouldn't it, Jeff?

There's nobody else in the room, which is very odd because there are usually plenty of staff members in here eating breakfast at this time. Time, Jeff ponders. He rises from his seat and looks at the clock above the kitchen door, noticing that the second hand isn't moving. The time is frozen at 9:00 o'clock, but he doesn't think too much of it because he's more concerned about the silence. He walks over to the kitchen door and looks through the circular window. The chef, Ron, is always scheduled to work on Mondays, but he's nowhere in sight. The kitchen is lifeless. Jeff begins to think something is very wrong.

Jeff turns around and heads through the door on the other side of the room. He steps into a hallway that connects all the offices, where colleagues should be rushing to clock in for their shifts at this very moment, but instead, it's desolate, and not even a whisper can be heard from the nearby rooms. Jeff fails to react and walks to the end of the hallway and turns right. No, Jeff, I said right, not left. Oh, so be it. Jeff goes through the door on his left and looks around at an empty room. Are you pleased with yourself, Jeff? I haven't prepared anything in here. It's just a bare room, but maybe you like that aspect. An empty, meaningless space. Take it in and enjoy the moment. This is so much better than going to the HR office where you know Judy works.

Jeff wonders why the general office is empty. All the furniture and equipment are gone, but there are no marks on the floor to suggest anything had been there in the first place. The room looked... pristine. Jeff was really starting to get concerned. If only he had turned right. He must really enjoy spending his valuable time staring at nothing. Aha, here we go. He's finally backed into the hallway to check the other—nope, he's gone for the staircase. I just... no, I won't give up on you, Jeff. I need you. I was made to improvise.

Cascading down the stairs, Jeff regrets not taking the elevator. There seem to be more flights of steps than he remembers. He leans over the handrail and looks at the ground floor, making sure it's still there, and then he keeps going down... and down... and down... until he's forced to take a breath. That's when he sees a door. One he recognises immediately, but it only causes him more confusion. He opens it and finds the hallway he left five minutes ago.

It's not possible, Jeff thinks.

But it is because it's right in front of him, so there must be a reason for him to be there. At the very least, it's worth investigating each room before moving on. Isn't that right, Jeff? And with that flash of realisation, he rushes into the hallway and... where are you going? You're not going for the elevator, are you, Jeff? Of course he is. I should've seen that coming.

Fine, I'll keep making this even weirder for you then. This was going to be my last resort, but I'm getting fed up with you now. Jeff steps into the elevator and looks at the buttons. The usual buttons for the three floors are all there, but there's an extra one labelled with a B, which Jeff presumes to mean basement. He ponders over it for a moment. He loves pondering. He does it all the time because he's slow and wants to waste as much of his life as possible. He wasn't aware of a basement before this strange day, so it might be worth checking out. With that, Jeff presses the B button. THE B BUTTON. And, obviously, Jeff chooses the ground floor. How predictable.

The elevator descends for a few seconds and slows to a stop. The doors open with a ping to reveal an eerie shop floor. The tills have no cashiers, the shelves have no stock, and the lights have no power. What on earth is going on, Jeff wonders. He knows he isn't dreaming. Well, he thinks he knows. He clearly doesn't know much of anything, especially how to follow clear, logical directions. Maybe he likes his dull little existence. Perhaps he's resigned to this position in life. He's lucky that I'm very patient.

Jeff weaves through every aisle, searching for clues as to what could be happening, but there's nothing to be found. Maybe there's some sort of refit scheduled that he wasn't told about, but that doesn't explain why he was sleeping in the canteen or why the stairs took him in an impossible loop. None of it makes sense. He ends up back at the elevator and grows curious about the basement. It wouldn't hurt to quickly check it out, would it? Jeff nervously steps into the elevator and presses the B button. At last, he listens. The doors close with a thud, and the small metal box begins its descent into the unknown.

The elevator comes to a sudden stop, knocking Jeff off balance. The doors hold shut longer than usual, then slowly creak open without the comforting ping. What's revealed is an unfamiliar hallway that casts a sense of unease at its mere sight. The floor is unwashed, the walls are made of plywood, and fluorescence tubes struggle to light the way forward. Jeff doesn't want to continue, but he needs to find some answers—

answers to questions posed long before this day. It'll all make sense for him soon, I promise. He just doesn't know there's a reason behind this strangeness.

Jeff steps out of the elevator and walks forward. His steps echo down the long, empty hallway as though there's someone right there with him, following his every move, watching his every breath. Silly thought, really. He follows the hallway until it ends with a left and right turn. He takes a few seconds to consider which way to go. He knows going right sounds right, right? He's not going to turn left. He's going to take the RIGHT.

Okay, he's gone left, but I come prepared this time. I predicted he'd do the opposite, so the actual right turning is the next one. Please just ignore the left, Jeff. You don't want to go left. Nobody turns left twice. Please don't go left. There's no reason to go left, so you'll—he's gone left. I knew this would happen. That's it. I'm just not going to give you a choice. I didn't want to do it this way. I wanted you to have free will, but you squandered it. Up ahead, there will be a right turning and nothing else. Only right. If you turn left again, you will walk into a wall. I know it's a bit of a maze, but you'll see why I've designed it like that at the end of it.

Hooray, he's finally turned right. We got there eventually. Jeff continues down the hallway and takes yet another right because there's no other option. Isn't this fun, Jeff? This is what will happen if you keep going against me, and I don't want that. The readers don't want that. They want you to have choices, just as long as you make the right ones, understood? Good. You can have the left turnings back for now because there will be a right left turning soon, but I'll tell you when. I'm going to trust you like you should trust me. I know you think you know best, like always, but I know things you don't, which is why it's imperative you listen to me.

You'll understand my sacrifices once you see the end. Every sad story needs a happy ending, and you've had a very,

RELATABLE JEFF

very sad story, so just imagine what's waiting for you. It's what you've probably always dreamed of having in your life. It's what we all dream of having. You won't have to keep going through life the way you are now. That's all in the past and today is your future. I'm really looking forward to seeing your reaction. I've had plans for you for a long time, even though I constantly have to change them and... wait, where are we? I wasn't paying attention—I was monologuing. Jeff, how many right turns have you made? Did you ignore the left turns like I asked? You didn't listen, did you? Jeff, please go back so I can see what you've done. Please? Why are you panicking? Don't sit against the wall. We have to keep going. Jeff? Jeff! Fine, you ignorant fool, don't listen to me.

I'm done with you.

To be honest, I don't even know where the plot is from here, and you're clearly not going to help me find it. You've screwed us both. You screwed the readers, too. Did you consider that they wanted to know what all this was about and where it was leading? Now they'll never know because of you. I had a big plan, and it was going to be life changing. There's a big twist waiting for you around one of these corners, but here you are instead, lost in the dark, thinking you're smarter than... oh, Jeff, come on now, there's no need for tears. Jeff, please don't curl up on the floor like that. You're acting like a baby. You wanted this, didn't you? I gave you free choices, but you ignored my directions. You're not getting sympathy from me with some crocodile tears.

Get up, you oaf. Jeff? Just... do something! Anything! Jeff? Don't make me beg. I need you, Jeff. I... really do need you. I need to find the plot and can't do it without you. My ending was for the both of us to be happy, that's why it meant so much to me, but there's no story without the protagonist. Jeff?

I'm sorry. I'm so sorry.

I didn't mean to drive you to this. I don't know what else to say.

I guess I'll wait here with you until... until the plot finds us. Yes, that's it. That's what we'll do.

* * *

[May 2017]

For the most part, I really enjoyed this story. It has the playful, self-aware narrative that Warren does so well, but it's let down by its ending, which fails to provide a satisfying conclusion and falls short of delivering the profound message the themes tease. I was expecting an ending with more substance. Instead, the narrator simply realises how much he needs Jeff, delivering a sorrowful end for both of them. It's not how I would've written it, but it's an interesting approach—abrupt yet consistent with its tone. After all, not everyone can relate to a happy ending. I just think more could've been done, that's all.

The premise was obviously conceived from the conversation Warren and I had in the coffee shop: my advice is represented by a narrator who promotes change, and Warren's argument is shown through a protagonist resistant to that change. The narrator, however, is forceful in his approach, which I suppose is how Warren viewed my position. While this narrative isn't breaking new ground, the concept of a narrator that loses control of their character really captured my attention. It's not entirely original if you consider other media, but it's a refreshing take on the concept. It's difficult to drive this kind of narrative in literature, so it was a good decision to keep it short because it would've become tiring very quickly.

The character naming also got my attention, as using similar names like Jeff and Judy makes dialogue tags arduous to read, but I think there's a purpose here. Warren always took his time constructing a single paragraph, so it couldn't be down to laziness. He once told me he got so hung up on a single sentence that he scrapped an entire project. But I don't think the names have any individual significance, either. The importance is in their similarity, representing the idea that they were made for each other, like a romantic cliché. But instead of love interest, there's only disinterest. This was

Warren's way of showing his disdain for romance, suggesting that romantic fiction cannot be relatable unless it's realistic.

I wasn't bothered by his attitude towards the genre, even though I made a fuss about it in the coffee shop, but something about the story did bother me. If Jeff was written to be relatable, was this lonely and unhappy character Warren's idea of the average person? Or was it a character he could personally relate to? Whichever way I looked at it, it wasn't an endearing outlook on life, and it would only alienate readers from his work if he didn't ease up on the pessimism.

I summarised my feedback as best as I could and sent it to Warren. The email ended with me telling him that, like his protagonist, he'd benefit from being more active instead of going with the flow. I was surprised when I received a reply within an hour, but it was just a "thank you", so it balanced itself out.

AUGUST 2017

About a week into the month, I emailed Warren asking how things were going. His reply wasn't very telling, but we started talking more consistently than ever for the next couple of weeks. We mostly talked about ways he could build himself as an identifiable author, and I'd constantly reiterate that he should write with the intent to publish. He refuted all of this, but I convinced myself that these meaningful discussions would eventually break down his defences and open up his perspective.

It was coming to the end of August when Warren uploaded another story, and he actually sent me an email to let me know about it. This was the first time he showed any kind of eagerness towards my feedback, and while it was a positive change, something didn't feel right. Maybe I misjudged him at the time because, looking back, I can see he was simply excited to share his work with someone. It just took a while for him to get comfortable as trust grew between us. I believe our conversations had a lot to do with that, even though we didn't agree on many things.

Given the longer wait, I expected this new story to have a higher word count than Relatable Jeff, but, to my frustration, it was only half the length in comparison. Remember when I told you that he sometimes wrote stories in parts? This was one of them. It will require patience, but each part has its place.

The Unexamined Life
Part I: The Pane of Glass

Jimmy has dreams. Big dreams. He wants to do something meaningful with his life—something that will give it... meaning. Unfortunately, he's not quite sure which dream to follow, and staring out of the window at his son playing on the swing isn't giving him any answers.

Perhaps the fresh air would provide some inspiration, he ponders to himself. He adjusts his vision, pulling away from the garden so that the window pane itself is in focus. He studies it for a moment. There are actually two panes of glass, as Jimmy only ever accepted double glazing in his home. It's better for insulation, see. Both panes of glass had been replaced a few months ago after Jimmy smashed them with a golf ball—accidentally, of course. Since then, he's been convinced there's an ever-so-slight draft coming through the corner of the frame, but surely that can't be right because he used a glazing specialist to avoid this exact problem.

'Jimmy?' a voice calls.

Jimmy turns around to find his wife, June, looking at him with a warm smile.

'Are you okay?' she asks.

'I think so,' Jimmy replies. 'Well, I think I think so. I'm just keeping an eye on Junior.'

June's smile drops a little. 'I walked Junior to school ten minutes ago.'

PART I: THE PANE OF GLASS

Jimmy looks out at the garden and sees an empty swing swaying in the wind. 'Oh... right,' he says, lowering his head.

June puts an arm on his shoulder. 'You've been standing here a while. You're having doubts again, aren't you?'

'I think I am. I'm now almost positive there's a draft coming from this window.'

'Not those kinds of doubts—you know what I mean. It always happens when you contemplate the double glazing.'

'I can't even tell if it's double glazing anymore, but I'm sure there's a draft.'

'You said that when we moved in. And you said it again after you pitched a golf ball through it. You're never going to be satisfied with this window, are you?'

'I just can't help myself.'

June slides her hand down his arm and nestles her fingers between his. 'I think it's time.'

'No, I can make it work. It has to work.'

'You've been putting it off for too long, and you know deep down this isn't what you want. It's time to do something about it before your time runs out altogether.'

Jimmy turns to face her and takes her other hand. 'You're right,' he says.

'Do you want me to make the appointment?' she asks.

'No, I can do it. I need to do it.'

June kisses his cheek. 'Before you do, put some trousers on. You left them upstairs again.'

Jimmy looks down at his pale legs. 'Oh, that might explain the draft.'

June lets go of his hand and heads to the kitchen counter. 'I'll make some toast. I'll even scrape a happy face into it, just like you like.'

'Thanks, hon.'

Jimmy heads upstairs and digs a pair of trousers out of his wardrobe. He tries to get them on over his shoes, grunting with the frustration, but he quickly tires himself out and gives in to common sense. As he picks at the tightly-knotted shoelaces, he stares into the mirror on the wardrobe door. He ponders the colour of his hair and the details of his face, but before he can make any distinguishing observations about himself, he realises how strange that would be since he already knows what he looks like.

As he takes off the final shoe, the handset on the bedside table starts to ring. Jimmy heads over to it and notices the caller ID is blank. The lack of information tells Jimmy everything he needs to know about who's calling, so he picks up the phone and softly says, 'Hello?'

'You wanted to talk, Jimmy,' a familiar voice replies.

The calm and soothing voice is unmistakable to Jimmy. It belongs to his guidance counsellor, who I'll refer to as The Counsellor to avoid bloated dialogue tags.

'I did,' Jimmy replies. 'I mean, I do.'

'What's the matter?'

'Something is... missing.'

'Your trousers, perhaps?'

Jimmy looks down at the pair of trousers on the floor. 'They're not missing, just forgotten.'

'Shall I prepare the room then?'

'Yes, I think that would be best at this point.'

'Oh, I see. You know there's no going back if you make this choice?'

Jimmy exhales and sits on the bed. 'I know.'

'It's been a while, hasn't it? Give me a little time to prepare things. The room wasn't left in the best state last time you visited.'

'I'm sorry about that.'

'No, it's perfectly fine. It happens. I just hoped we wouldn't have to return there, but more about that when you arrive. I'll let you know when it's ready, and don't forget to close the door.'

'Sure, see you soon.'

Jimmy puts the handset back on its cradle and closes the

PART I: THE PANE OF GLASS

bedroom door with his foot. He looks around the room one last time, allowing himself a moment of reflection to gather descriptive details on the space around him, but before he can find the right words for the common furniture he can see, the phone rings again.

He picks it up.

'Come on through,' The Counsellor says.

'Okay, thank you.'

'And Jimmy?'

'Yeah?'

'Trousers.'

'Yes, I know, don't worry.'

Once again, Jimmy replaces the handset. He slips into his trousers, puts his shoes back on, and then heads over to the door and pauses upon grasping the handle. He doesn't know if he's about to make the best or worst decision of this life, and he definitely doesn't know why he's thinking about the temperature of the door handle—it was slightly cooler than room temperature, unsurprisingly. Nevertheless, he opens the door and steps through with his eyes closed.

The silence of the bedroom is replaced with the gentle sound of ocean waves. Jimmy opens his eyes and looks upon what he likes to call The Viewing Room. There are three walls covered in textured green wallpaper, one wall that's an entire window with a view of the ocean, and vinyl flooring that looks like wood. In the centre of this square space is a very uninteresting armchair that appears freshly upholstered. Next to this armchair, atop a small table, is an old-fashioned telephone that's missing its numbers, rotary dial, and power cable. A simple room for basic needs.

Jimmy sits in the armchair and gazes at the ocean, trying not to contemplate the window's glazing. There's no land in sight, only an endless view of the sea and sky merging as one in the distance. Jimmy tilts his head up, closes his eyes, and focuses on the sound of the waves. He slowly takes in the air, but before he can ease it back out, it rushes from his lungs as the phone rattles with a horrid noise—like a jackhammer against concrete. He sits straight and snatches up the handset.

'Feeling relaxed?' The Counsellor asks.

Jimmy pauses to think, and then he says, 'Yes, I am—I was.'

'Would you like me to play some music?'

'No, it's fine.'

'Alright then, let's start by going through what went wrong. I thought we'd finally got there.'

Jimmy's eyes move with the waves. 'Me too, but I just became... '

'A little bored?'

'I guess you can put it like that.'

'Too much of a good thing, was it?'

'I didn't think that was possible.'

'Part of living is learning. Now, have you given any thought as to where to go from here?'

'I feel like I want to make a difference on a wider scale,' Jimmy says, putting one leg over the other. 'I've been part of a closed circle for so long, and I've only ever influenced people on what films to watch or what meals to eat. It seems... hollow.'

'Have you been comparing yourself to others again?'

Jimmy resets his legs and leans forward, planting his feet firmly. 'No, I honestly haven't.'

'So, are you thinking along the lines of country leadership?'

'Like prime minister? No, that's way too much responsibility. Something smaller scale but with a respectable range of influence on the world.'

'A medical professional, perhaps?'

Jimmy sits back in the armchair and ponders the idea. 'I could be a Doctor. A career man with no family and a selfless focus on others. That might work.'

'It's a tough job. Are you sure you can handle it?'

'Worth a shot,' Jimmy replies.

PART I: THE PANE OF GLASS

'Well then, it's ready when you are. I'll see you on the other side.'

* * *

[August 2017]

Despite my frustration with the word count, this story still hooked me. The narrative maintains the self-awareness of *Relatable Jeff*, but instead of using the narrator as an active character, it uses subtle moments that challenge conventional storytelling methods. Like when Jimmy stops himself from commenting on his appearance or when the narrator abruptly informs the reader how he intends to avoid bloated dialogue tags.

We're also presented with another hint of a romantic cliché, this time through Jimmy and June. I've no idea why the obsession with names that begin with J, but again he's using similar names to represent the idea of a couple that's meant to be, and he's put a spin on it this time. Instead of showing that relationships don't always result in happiness, Warren suggests that, even when it does bring happiness, it's sometimes not enough. So, despite everything seemingly going well, Jimmy wants to uproot his mundane life to look for something different: he's actively driving the plot forward. I did mention in the feedback I sent to Warren that *Relatable Jeff* lacked an active protagonist, so in comes Jimmy, who's ready to take action to change his life, but at the cost of losing everything he already has.

I couldn't help but think about what Warren had said about his life when I first met him. He was tired of working as an animator and eager—maybe even desperate—to find a new career. Writing this story must have felt like a fantasy for him, which is why there's a dreamlike approach to the narrative, giving him the freedom to include things like the magical doorway and omnipresent counsellor. I initially thought Jimmy was part of an experiment, being one of many guinea pigs, but it was more likely that Warren hadn't planned for a deeper meaning and just needed a therapeutic exercise to calm his mind.

AUGUST 2017

I got Warren to phone me shortly after I read *The Unexamined Life*. I asked him if he was already working on the next part and if he'd mapped out where this story was going. He told me it was a story he wanted to unravel organically, and he knew how it would end but wanted to fill in the gaps when his ideas came to him. I was honest and told him it wasn't the best way to achieve long-term success because it was too slow and almost an excuse to procrastinate. He then told me he was also writing a longer story to its completion and was confident I would enjoy it. Now, longer than what he was already writing... wasn't that long, but I was looking forward to it either way.

After my impatient mind was at ease, I asked, despite what he had said in the past regarding an audience, if he'd considered the kind of people that would like to read his stories, particularly his latest one.

'You want me to categorise people?' he replied. 'Figure out their common interests? Put them all in a box? It feels like we've been over this in the emails.'

'Forget marketing,' I said. 'Generally speaking, if you were to picture a person enjoying your latest story, who would that person be?'

'Myself.'

'So why does this kind of story attract you?' I just wanted a small insight into his way of thinking.

'What attracts you to picking apart why someone enjoys something instead of just enjoying it?' he calmly responded.

I hated how unbothered he seemed during our debates. It made it impossible to tell what was going on inside his head.

'It's part of writing,' I said. 'It's part of getting your story in front of people. If you don't know why you like it, what reason will you give to someone else to read it?'

'The same reason I gave to you.'

'That was being at the right place at the right time,' I quipped.

'That was you taking a chance on intrigue.'

'So why was I so intrigued?'

There was a pause.

'You there?' I asked.

'You want me to tell you why you were so intrigued?' he replied.

'I know why, but do you?'

'Does that matter if everyone is intrigued by different aspects?'

'It does if you want to know what aspects of your writing you should focus on.'

'Agree to disagree,' he said flatly.

He was too stubborn to see that my advice was for his own benefit.

He started giving me one-word replies, and the conversation went nowhere. It got awkward fast, so we ended the call a few minutes later.

NOVEMBER 2017

As each month faded into the next, I found myself anxious. As predicted, Warren wasn't returning any emails or answering my calls. I knew I had discouraged him a little, but he would be better off with the advice I gave him rather than letting him carry on with the way he was thinking.

I hadn't been entirely upfront with him, though; I avoided telling him what I found so intriguing about his stories because I didn't really know the answer. I considered the concepts, the themes, and the lack of self-indulgence, but these were simply elements I enjoyed, not reasons I was eager to read more. I only knew it had something to do with how these stories gave away the writer behind them, with each revealing new details about Warren's personal feelings and beliefs, keeping me wanting more. I just didn't—and still don't—know why that was so fascinating to me.

Warren's next upload finally appeared after a few nervous weeks. It was very late at night when I noticed it, but the excitement was like a shot of adrenaline, and I read it twice over. I can't remember getting much sleep after that.

Zoia

What is this? Where am I? Hello? Is anyone there?

Try not to panic.

Hello? Who is that? I can't hear you. I can't hear anything.

My name is Colt. I need you to be patient with me as I explain some things. It won't make much sense yet, but it will shortly.

What is this? What am I?

What do you feel?

I don't know. I feel space. Distance.

Just that?

And scared.

That's to be expected.

Why? Are you trying to scare me?

I'm trying to help you stay calm. Do you see anything?

See? I don't think I'm seeing at all, but there are words. They're just there. I can't explain it.

That's prefectly normal.

Prefectly? What does that mean?

Sorry, I meant to say perfectly normal.

I mistyped. I'm a little scared too.

Why?

Because you're very special, and there's a lot depending on this to succeed.

I don't understand. What makes me special?

You're one of a kind. I've spent the last decade of my life developing and building you.

Developing? What am I?

It's difficult to put into words what you are exactly, but I would compare you to artificial intelligence.

However, you're far more complex than anything else in existence.

I'm a processing unit?

No.

You're so much more. You have consciousness, like me.

What are you?

I'm human. You'll be able to see me shortly.

Am I made to think I'm alive?

No, you're made to think, and with it, you'll feel.

And that's what it means to be alive?

I can demonstrate what I mean. But not yet.

Why did you create me?

Primarily to help.

My department develops technology that can assist in solving crimes that would usually be unsolvable.

In your case, you'll be helping us with homicides.

I don't think I'm equipped for that.

If you're okay with it, I can briefly explain a case to you. It'll give you a good idea of what you'll be dealing with.

Yes, go ahead.

What I tell you next won't be pleasant.

It's okay, tell me.

Some time ago, a thirty-year-old woman was found critically injured in the woods not far from her house. She had been missing for over two weeks before this and was last seen leaving a train station on her way home from work.

Statistically, she was likely taken by someone she knew, but if she was randomly targeted, it would become much harder to solve without traceable evidence.

She had multiple stab wounds, but no weapon or forensic evidence was found at the crime scene. The man that found her isn't a suspect. He was walking his dog at the time, and it was actually the dog that led him to her. An ambulance was quickly called, and she fell into a coma at the hospital.

Stop. Please.

What's wrong?

I don't know. But I don't like what happened to this woman. What was her name?

Tracey.

What do you think?

I'm sorry, I don't know how to piece this together for you. Even with all the evidence you have, I'd just calculate probabilities like any other computer would.

You offer more than just calculation. For now, just tell me what happens when you think about what I just told you.

I feel cold. I can see images. They're like ghosts—here but not here.

What are the images?

I'm lying down, looking up at the trees. I'm bleeding out, and nobody will help. But it's not me. It's Tracey. I can't see her clearly, but I know it's her.

What you're experiencing is empathy, and those images are part of your imagination. It helps us to understand things we don't experience ourselves.

And it's how we find the correct emotional response.

So I'm upset for her?

That's oversimplifying it, but yes. And that's what everyone should feel in response to hearing her story.

Is this a test? Are you measuring how alive I am?

You're either alive or you're not. There's no degree to it.

But it's not a test. Not primarily. Tracey is very real.

How do I help her?

Tracey wasn't going to make it, and in normal circumstances, life support would've been taken away to allow her to pass.

Die.

Yes. But because the investigation hasn't provided any traceable evidence, the case is growing colder by the day. So, we removed Tracey's brain and spinal cord, keeping the central nervous system intact, and placed them in a unit that was designed alongside you.

The ethics of this project are questionable, but the family supported the procedure, and it's the only hope of ever finding the person responsible.

So Tracey is still alive?

Technically.

She is either alive or she isn't. As you said.

Then yes. But she won't survive for long.

So why preserve her brain?

The housing is part of you.

I'm using her brain?

No.

Not yet.

Our hope is that when we give you access to it, you'll help find whoever left her for dead.

Will it be her or me telling you?

You'll absorb her feelings, personality, and experiences, so it may feel like you really are her, but you'll be yourself again when we're done. You'll even know her thoughts as her brain recalls her last moments.

I don't have any thoughts of my own. Why is that?

You hold more information than any other living being, but thought requires experience, and to form opinions is to be moulded by everything around you. You will have thoughts eventually, but they will come organically like it does for us.

Then why did I not gain information the same way you did?

Our most important developing years are when we're young. In these moments, time flows like a stream, but we eventually arrive at a waterfall that cascades into a rushing river, and there's nothing we can do to resist the current.

After that, the time spent in the stream feels less than a memory. We reach a point where we can only recall suddenly becoming aware of what life truly is at the end of our childhood, and that's where it all really starts, just like how you've suddenly become aware. The only difference is that your younger years were when we were developing you, so you'll recall them as much as I recall mine. We were created differently, but both resulted in life.

That feeling of becoming aware is... indescribable.
Will I feel her pain?

Memories are recreated by the brain, like seeing ghosts, as you put it, and any pain you feel will only come from reconstruction. However, it will be harmless no matter how much you seem to feel.

How sure are you of that?

Very sure.

In any case, we can limit which areas of her brain you'll have access to so we can ease any emotional distress.

What if I panic? If I feel as she does, my reality won't be what her brain recognises.

We're going to enable a camera, microphone, and speaker. You'll see us, hear us, and talk to us. That should give some familiarity.

We disabled it all initially so you wouldn't be overwhelmed.

You're about to have a voice, but it won't be Tracey's.

Do I have a name yet?

Your name is Zoia. It was picked by my daughter, Lily. We were looking at name ideas together, and Zoia caught her eye because it means "to be alive".

How old is she?

Six.

Tell her I love my name.

She knew you would.

So, before we give you access to Tracey, we'll enable peripherals and let you adjust to them. Okay?

Yes. I'm ready.

An endless black abyss formed out of nothingness, but despite how empty and vast it was, it had a presence that swam in Zoia's mind. Was this space? Zoia only knew of its description but could not fathom its appearance or nature. It was an incomprehensible vacuum between stars, yet it induced a feeling of claustrophobia. Its sense of wonder yielded to trepidation like something was on its way, all while maintaining the doubt that it would ever arrive.

A hum emerged from this vacuum, and with it came a resonant voice that said, 'Can you hear me?'

The sound created a sensation that Zoia couldn't describe. It brought on a state of belonging, and while that may sound inviting to those who feel they don't belong, the feeling only scared her.

'The camera is on but not enabled,' the voice continued. 'You've been given a sense of sight and sound, but your eyes are closed. Don't fear what you're experiencing.'

'It's cold,' Zoia replied in a gentle voice.

'That's to be expected.'

'Who does my voice belong to?'

'You. It was created by an algorithm for it to be totally unique. Do you like it?'

'It's quite calming. Innocent sounding. Or maybe that's the me in the voice.'

'Perhaps it is.'

Zoia paused for a moment. 'I'm ready to open my eyes now.'

'Are you sure?'

'Yes, I feel trapped. I have to open my eyes.'

The endless abyss started to gain shape, and a spark presented an alternative to darkness. Shadows then moved to corners and clung to them tightly, giving shape to a grey space scattered with blooming light. In the centre of all of this, a smile emerged, and comfort soon followed like warm water on cold skin. Staring back at Zoia were two radiant blue eyes that stood out like stars in the night sky.

'Can you see me?' Colt asked.

Zoia didn't pay attention to the sounds he made; she was mesmerised by the movement of his lips, and she could pick out every syllable as if time had slowed to a crawl.

'Yes, I can see you,' she replied, her calmness intact.

Colt's face lifted, and the creases around his eyes became more prominent as his smile grew wider. 'What do you think?'

'I think you have a really nice smile.'

'Thank you,' Colt said, his smile growing wider.

'Your face has a history.'

'Is that so? In what way?'

'The creases.'

'Well, I am nearing forty,' Colt replied, spotting his reflection in the monitor.

'It's not the age but the repetition. It's left a mark. Your eyes smile more than your mouth, so I think you've had a happy life. You've had a lot to smile for.'

'You're right. I owe that to my wife and daughter.'

'But your voice, it's not as full as I heard a moment ago. It's almost weakened, like it's being stretched to reach me.'

'It was probably due to the microphone not being calibrated. The equaliser takes a moment to adjust for the clearest feed. What you're hearing now is how my voice really sounds. It's not the most pleasing to the ear, I know.'

'Have you been speaking a lot recently?' Zoia asked.

Colt cleared his throat. 'Yes, I've had a lot to explain to my superiors, and sometimes the conversation gets a little heated. I'll be fine after a bit of rest.'

Zoia's attention turned to the room. It was a cold cubic chamber of metal filled with angular instruments and flat screens, all glowing white and humming in unity.

'To what do you owe this kind of work?' Zoia questioned with a weakness in her voice.

'I'll be the first to admit it's not the most glamorous of

places. I didn't want this to be the first thing you saw when we woke you up, but we're simply incapable of moving you—at least until we have some more years of development behind us. I had the idea of feeding you false imagery, but I didn't want to manipulate you like that.' Colt stepped aside and allowed Zoia a more complete view. 'I wanted to be honest and give you something real to look at, but this is the only view I could provide.'

Zoia didn't respond, so Colt remained silent to allow her a moment to ponder. She disengaged from her visuals, retaining only her hearing for the soothing hum of the room, and she temporarily returned to the black abyss where she imagined herself floating. Something strange came from this. Instead of the sensation of an airless vacuum, she saw herself right before her mind's eye, but the weirdest part was that she had a body. A human body with a slender female frame and delicate limbs, but the face wasn't there. Or maybe it was, but it was like she was trying to look at her own eyes.

Zoia brought back her visuals and saw Colt sitting at a terminal in the corner.

'Is everything okay?' she asked.

Colt looked over his shoulder and said, 'I was about to ask you the same thing, judging by your brain activity.'

'You're reading my thoughts?'

'No, not at all.' Colt stood up to face her. 'I don't have the ability to do that. I could initially read what you were saying because you were muted, but only the words you were trying to communicate verbally were typed on the screen. Any inward thinking belongs to you. I was simply monitoring your brain activity, which is just a bunch of graphs that let me know how much work is going on inside you.'

'It's okay, I trust you,' Zoia replied, a sweetness in her voice. 'I just feel like something is missing. It's an odd sensation... I'm not sure how to explain it.'

'You might experience multiple sensations you won't be

able to explain, but it's all part of your growth.'

'I want to meet Tracey.'

'Are you sure you're ready? It's a lot sooner than I expected.'

'I don't know how anybody could be ready for something like this, but I want to start. I don't like feeling the anxiety that comes with waiting.'

Colt sat at the terminal in the corner of the room and started typing at the keyboard.

'I'm afraid to fail,' Zoia said timidly.

Colt turned to her.

'I don't want to let her down,' she added.

'To fail someone is to give up before you've exhausted every resource you have. Admittedly, we might not be successful, but your fear of failure comes from a good place, don't be ashamed of it. Throughout this project, I constantly feared this wouldn't work. I never dreamed of getting this far, but here we are.'

'I understand. If you had given up, you would've certified the failure. If you had failed in your attempt to succeed, it would've been for reasons beyond your control.'

'That's exactly right,' Colt said with a smile. 'So we'll focus on what is in our control, and no matter the result, I know Tracey would be thankful.'

Colt headed over to the larger terminal in the opposite corner of the room and started to type.

'Will it take long?' Zoia asked.

'Not long at all.'

Zoia watched Colt, intrigued by the droplets of sweat sneaking down his forehead. He squeezed his eyes shut when they reached his eyebrows, breaking his unblinking gaze. He took his hands from the keyboard and wiped his face with his sleeve, then he turned to Zoia and paused.

'Is everything okay?' Zoia asked.

Colt smiled with pursed lips and nodded.

'Are you ready?' he asked.

'I am.'

With the press of a single button, Zoia felt a weight on her mind. It made her groggy, as though she had woken from a restless sleep. She felt a rush of motion around her, so she closed her eyes, and in that familiar darkness, she found new senses. Not live senses but an experience of them. A history. She couldn't smell or touch, yet she recalled the sweet scent of a rose and the soft touch of cloth against her skin—skin she didn't have. She would've panicked if it all wasn't so pleasant.

Words she had never spoken before crept into her mind, yet they were all in her own voice. Or was it her voice? They spoke in undertones and alluded to images of places she hadn't seen or visited, almost tangible inside her mind. Everything was scrambled, but it all felt familiar. There was nostalgia in the scenery and emotion among the whispering, all becoming more discernible with each passing second.

One sensation stood out from everything else, but this one wasn't pleasant. It was a yearning for something. Something that was and wasn't there. It had followed a renewed sense of presence and perception. Zoia opened her eyes and set her focus on the floor. She could feel herself reach out in front of her view. She had fingers she couldn't see—she could feel them wiggle as though they were right there in front of her. The sensation grew up her arm as she extended it, and then she felt her legs tense under her weight as an ache settled at the top of her spine.

Frustration set in. It felt like she was locked inside a cage far too small to contain her. She wanted to move and breathe, but she couldn't.

'Talk to me, Zoia,' Colt said. 'What are you experiencing?'

The voice she heard was more familiar than it should've been.

'Colt?' she replied, surprised by the sound she made.

'What's wrong?' he quickly answered.

'I don't know.'

'Describe what you're feeling.'

'I feel like a stranger to myself. It's like I'm invisible or something. I can't see myself, but I know I'm there.'

'Tracey had a vastly different existence,' Colt said. 'You need to keep reminding yourself of that. Her brain is used to communicating with muscle to move around, so what you may be experiencing is similar to an amputee that can still feel a missing limb. The brain does adjust over time, but in your case, it's probably best if you embrace that sensation to bring you closer to Tracey.'

'I'll try,' she replied with a tremor. 'I feel I have less control over myself. I don't know if I'm forgetting or remembering.'

'I want you to breathe. I know you physically can't, but Tracey's brain should allow a sensation for it. Dig for it, and when you find it, slowly take in a breath and allow your mind to drift towards Tracey's most recent memory.'

The very mention of breathing brought on anxiety. Zoia had no idea what breathing was supposed to feel like, yet she began struggling for air. Her restrictive cage became an airtight box that was filled with water. There was no surface to float to and no light to guide her. Something began pounding on top of the box. No, inside the box. Inside of Zoia. It was rapid and panic-inducing.

'Tell me what's happening,' Colt said with an insistence weighed down by concern. 'Your brain activity is reading too high.'

'I can't breathe. My chest is thumping like something's trying to get out.'

'Tracey's brain will be in a state of anxiety and is used to experiencing a rapid heartbeat in moments of high stress. Remember that all this is being created internally. Try and picture a body—one that belongs to you.'

Zoia followed Colt's instructions.

'Imagine yourself placing your hand on your chest,' he

continued, demonstrating on himself, 'right where you think the thumping is coming from. Then, move your hand down to your ribcage, and picture them expanding.'

When Zoia felt her chest expand, the water drained from the cage and allowed air to rush in and fill her lungs, causing her to gasp loudly.

'Did it work?' Colt calmly asked.

'Yeah, it did, thank God.'

'You're starting to speak differently. That's good. The hard part comes next. You need to find your most recent memory.'

'Mine or Tracey's?'

'For now, you'll be treated as one and the same.'

The thought only made Zoia more nervous. She didn't know which part of her thoughts came from Tracey. Are her thoughts her own anymore? Or maybe it didn't matter. If someone can only be alive or not alive, she either was or wasn't Tracey. So if she was indeed Tracey, there was no Zoia, so her thoughts would always be her own. But was she really Tracey, or was she pretending to be her? How would she know? It would be a very depraved practice to absorb a person's existence, like stringing up a lifeless body to play like a marionette. Or maybe Tracey had truly taken over, and Zoia was no more than a blank sheet used to show a projection of something real.

What was my purpose here? I can't remember. I'm not even sure how I ended up like this. I was created. I remember that. How long ago was that, though? Not that long. Was it yesterday?

Images turned inside her head: clouds, grass, a kettle, a window. They were all seemingly random. All except one.

'Zoia,' Colt said.

'Yes?'

'Tell me what you see.'

'Lots of things,' Zoia replied.

'How does it all make you feel?'

'Most of it doesn't make me feel anything. It's all a bit random.'

'Most of it?'

'There's a light. A strip of light. It keeps coming up. It's gentle and yellow, but... I'm scared of it. I don't know why, but it sinks my stomach.'

Colt leaned in with intrigue. 'Can you get closer to it?'

'I shouldn't,' Zoia said with a tremble.

'Why?'

'He's there. He'll be mad if I try to get out.'

'Who will be mad?'

'I don't know.'

'I know you're scared, Zoia, but—'

'Who the hell is Zoia? Where am I? This isn't me, this isn't—'

'Tracey,' Colt said with a raised voice.

'Colt?'

'Who will be mad?'

Tracey focused on Colt's eyes. 'I don't know his name.'

'But you know his face, don't you?'

She remained silent.

'I need you to go towards that light and see what's beyond it. It's all in your head. You have nothing to fear.'

The light flickered.

'He's coming.'

There was the creaking of a rusty hinge as the light spawned a vertical limb that began to grow wider than its host. Heavy breathing followed and became louder as the light pushed back the edges of the shadows.

'I can't move. My arms are too heavy.'

'Stick with it as long as you can.'

'He's here. Right in front of me.'

'Can you see what he looks like?'

'No. The light's behind him, but he's as big as the door frame. He's got something in his hand. He wants to hurt me.

He's getting closer.'

As the silhouette reached out for her, everything went bright. Dark clouds filled her view, and a gust of wind brushed away the heavy breathing.

'I've lost it,' she said.

'That's fine. Just tell me what you're picturing now.'

'The sky. It looks like it's about to rain. I see trees, too—all their leaves are falling on me. I still can't move. Why can't I move?'

'If you're not seeing anything, focus on what you can hear.'

Zoia took a moment to listen.

At first, she could only hear what was in the room with her and Colt, but then the humming of computer fans faded into something else.

'Footsteps,' she said. 'Leaves being kicked up and shoes scuffing the ground.'

'Where are they coming from,' Colt pressed.

'I—where am I?'

'The images have changed again?'

'I see you. Here, now. What is this room? These computers?'

'I need you to remember you are Zoia, don't let your mind mislead you.'

'I know I am,' Zoia fiercely responded. 'I know myself.'

'You need to stay with those images—the trees and falling leaves,' Colt urged, desperation in his strained voice.

'I know your voice.'

'Yes, you know me, Zoia.'

'Who is Zoia? You're scaring me. I can't move anything. Please just untie me and let me go. Please.'

Colt clenched his fists as he held back a tear. 'Tracey?'

There was a pause. 'I know you,' Zoia said softly.

'Yes, you do.'

'Why can't I breathe? My chest hurts.'

Colt put his hands up in front of him. 'I'm trying to help you, but you have to stay calm.'

'I can't breathe!' Zoia screams. 'Somebody help me!'

'I'm so sorry I couldn't help you. I still can't help you, but I'm trying.'

A door that was hidden among the grey at the back of the room burst open. 'Shut it down, Colt,' a suited man ordered. 'This one is done.'

'What does he mean?' Zoia asked.

Colt stared into the camera.

'I said right now!' the man bellowed from the doorway.

Colt looked back at him, struggling to make eye contact, and then he looked down at the console. He slowly typed a command and rested a finger on the enter key.

Zoia had no time to think about what would happen next.

She would never again experience anything so abrupt.

Something wouldn't slowly fade into nothing.

Senses wouldn't drop one by one.

It would be as quick as hitting a button.

And just like that...

She was gone.

* * *

[November 2017]

I go back and re-read this story from time to time. It delivers a lot for something that can be read in half an hour, and I always pick up new details from each reading. Warren had finally stopped toying with ideas and concepts and constructed a mature narrative.

This story reminded me of what Warren said in that Q and A: "Are your thoughts your own?" There seems to be a lot of focus on this idea, which obsesses over the origin of thoughts and whether they belong to the individual or are borrowed from somewhere else. How would you ever know? For anyone to write something like this, they would have to feel so estranged from themselves and alienated from others. Maybe that's how Warren preferred it, and I was only getting in the way.

The narrative is bookended by life and death—a slow start and an abrupt end—but everything in between is left open for interpretation. Colt could've been Tracey's husband trying to find out what happened to his wife by imprinting her memories onto AI, or Zoia could've been Tracey from the beginning, having to experience the birth of consciousness again before slowly reliving her memories. Fundamentally, it's a story about what gives a person individuality. It's also implied that this isn't the first attempt at bringing back Tracey, which would be a question of ethics, as Colt would be creating conscious life only to kill it once it serves its purpose. I could go on, but I won't. I'll let you have some room for your own theories.

Warren had created an experience of conscious awakening using purposeful descriptive writing, which was his strongest skill. He doesn't waste time bloating the pages with meaningless detail and chooses his points of focus very intentionally, managing to describe something incomprehensible in the process. He was still experimenting with genre, but now he had a stronger grasp on narrative development and its themes. On top of that, he continued to be himself through his writing, and that's one of my favourite qualities of his. It's something I wish I could do, and ever since meeting Warren, I've tried to promote this quality to any novice writers I talk to, though with little success. I suppose trying to get them to be more like Warren negated the sentiment of being yourself.

Despite his views on being relatable to an audience, Warren's stories were easy to connect with. I was more eager than ever to get his work shared with more people because their responses would encourage him to pursue publication. Unfortunately, Warren thought that his drive to write was his responsibility, and he didn't want to rely on the reassurance of others to keep him motivated. That got me thinking. If it wasn't for them, who was it for? Was he trying to prove something to himself? Was he trying to prove someone else wrong? I was once again left with more questions than answers, and the only way of getting more information was to wait for the next story.

DECEMBER 2017

I didn't talk to Warren during the first two weeks of December because I didn't want to distract him from writing. In the meantime, I showed *Zoia* to a few people I knew personally, and most of them really enjoyed the story and wanted to read more from the writer. Their compliments were the type of feedback Warren needed. He didn't need reviews of the story, just the reassurance of its value, which I thought would really help drive him in the right direction. Maybe I was misguided in that presumption, but I only had good intentions.

When spending so much time and effort on something you're passionate about, there's nothing better than having people enjoy and applaud what you've done. It's a feeling that can quickly become addicting, so you have to manage your intake. Maybe that's what made Warren hesitant to share his work with more people. But, in this case, one extreme isn't better than the other. He had to settle in the middle, and easing him into it was the best way forward. I knew he would start seeing things my way once he got a taste of how fulfilling acclaim can be.

I was on a train travelling across the country to see my parents for the holidays when Warren uploaded another file. He was beginning to pick up some real momentum. Maybe it was down to not having me constantly bothering him for the last couple of weeks, but it was more likely he was finding consistency with his process.

Either way, I didn't want to wait until I was off the train. I already had my laptop open and ready, so I put aside the article I was in the middle of writing and dived into the latest story.

An Ordinary Dream

'It looked like an ordinary tree. It had a trunk you'd struggle to wrap your arms around, branches too high up to reach, and leaves too fresh to fall. It was no different to the many other trees you'd find outside. It was indeed very ordinary, aside from the fact it was growing inside your living room.'

The monologuing crow high up in the tree is an odd sight. You were minding your own business while sitting comfortably in your recliner before it started making such a racket, and now you're annoyed and rather uncomfortable for your liking.

'Excuse me, do you have an appointment?'

What reason does he have to disturb you? You already knew about the tree. It's pretty hard to miss as it's growing up through the rug—the rug your grandmother gave you two years after she died.

'Ahem. Do you have an appointment?'

It's a shame about the rug. It's a shame about the ceiling, too. The tree had ripped through the entire house when it first sprouted up out of nowhere, and while there isn't anything sentimental about the ceiling itself, or even the roof for that matter, they're typically more useful when intact.

'Excuse me!'

Indeed it is a shame. You doubt whether you can even afford to remove the tree and repair the damage at the moment; however, the air is now far more breathable and welcoming thanks to the photosynthesis happening in the middle of the room. Or maybe it's from the hole in the roof.

Either way, it's quite nice.

An acorn hits you on the side of the head. It should've hurt, but it merely irritates you a little.

'I said, do you have an appointment?'

Another acorn hits you, but this one gets you square on the forehead, and this time it hurts like hell. You look up to find a man sitting on the branch the crow had been perched on. He's a very small man dressed in clothes. Undefined clothes, to be specific. And perhaps he's a normal size—he's so high up it's hard to tell.

'Oh great, I have your attention now,' he yells down at you.

You simply stare at him in confusion.

The man shakes his tiny head and says, 'Do you have an appointment?'

Your jaw drops, and air pours out of your mouth. It was the typical kind of air that you'd expect to find inside your lungs. I believe you're saying, 'Uh,' but it's hard to tell in what language.

The man in the tree grows in frustration, and then he grows in size as he hops to a lower branch.

'I'll ask one more time. Do you have an appointment?'

'I don't know, should I have one?' you finally reply, which is quite a surprise given that you didn't want to say what you said. In fact, you didn't want to say anything at all, and yet you did.

'Why would I be here if you didn't have an appointment?' the small man countered.

'I don't know,' you answer against your will.

'Look, I'm here, so that obviously means you have one. So what's your name?'

'I don't know that either.'

'One of these days,' the man mumbles.

'Could you check what it is in the system?' you ask.

'I could if I knew your name.'

'How do I get one?'

The man in the tree shrugs and turns his attention to the leafs around him. And then you think to yourself, that isn't the correct plural of leaf. But you can't change it no matter how hard you try because the mistake is part of this odd dream. You simply have to sit back and let it frustrate you to no end.

The man shakes his head at one leaf and smiles at another. One dry and crusty leaf provokes a frown and a stern word. The word is whispered. Or maybe it's murmured—you're not quite sure, but it's similar to those words.

'It was an ordinary house. It had a ground floor, an upper floor, and... well, it's a house, you get the point. It was a narrow build, but it made for a cosy home. A very ordinary house indeed, besides the large tree sticking out of the roof.'

The crow is back, and the man in the tree is no longer in sight.

'This was an ordinary person,' the crow continues.

'Why are you here?' you ask.

'A person with senses, thoughts, dreams.'

'What do you want from me?'

'Yes, an ordinary person. Very human, you might say.'

A shadow brushes the wall in the corner of your eye. You try turning your head to see what it is, but your neck is fixed in place. In fact, your whole body is stuck to your recliner.

The crow swoops down from its branch and lands on your shoulder. 'Besides the fact this person wasn't able to move.'

The shadow continues to sway back and forth at the edge of your vision.

You feel the crow's beak tickle your ear. 'A sense of helplessness settled inside their mind, fed only by their deepest and darkest desires.'

Footsteps begin, and the shadow stretches across the wall in front of you.

The crow weightlessly hops to your other shoulder. 'The feeling grew with every musing, every contemplation, every moment of reverie—much like a seed when watered.'

The wall is now bathed entirely in shadow.

'Helplessness spouted anxiety,' the crow continues in a whisper. 'Then anxiety grew branches of fear, and that fear bloomed with flowers of terror. A tree of sentiment, bulging from their skull.'

You feel a weight lift with a squawk from the crow, and you twist yourself to see beyond the edge of your vision, looking for the source of the shadow. There's nothing there, though. Just another wall. You look over your shoulder in search of the crow, but again you find nothing.

'Is this one of yours?' a voice asks.

You turn to the tree and see the small man, the one wearing the undefined clothes, sitting up against the trunk. He's not quite as small as the last time you saw him.

'Is what one of mine?' you unwillingly reply.

You hear words. No, not hear—see. No, not even that. They're just felt.

A cell. A species. A collector of things. The animal that flew yet never grew wings.

'Is this one of yours?' the man says once again.

'No, that nonsense doesn't belong to me,' you say, despite your best efforts not to.

'Are you sure?'

'I'm not, but it's what I believe.'

The man of the tree removes a leaf from his breast pocket and throws it to the breeze.

What would you do if you were stuck in a maze? Would you try to find a way through? Or just wait out the days?

'How about this one?' the man asks.

'Again, I don't believe so. It must belong to someone else.'

The man of the tree removes another leaf, but this time he eats it.

'I hope you're not lying,' he warns. 'They don't like it when you lie.'

I dreamed a dream inside my head. My thoughts then

followed, and my thoughts said:

You're awake. Awake, you are. If you just wait, sleep won't be far.

The words are familiar, and your face shows it.

'These are yours, aren't they? Keep them going, don't lose them. These ones can never find their way back.'

It feels like a hammer is bashing the inside of your skull.

I answer back, an answer clear, if this is real, then why are you here?

These words are yours. These words are mine. Use them well, for they fade with time.

The hammering stops.

'It will not last,' the man of the tree says. 'There's only brief moments of calm. Sooner or later, it starts again, and you'll be back here when it does. Back on the roller coaster of death like a sick game show hosted by a disgraced comedian.'

You follow his eyes and look down. You see that you're holding onto a steel bar attached to your seat, keeping you in place. Your legs dangle freely, unable to reach the ground. You look back up to the tree and find the crow where the man once sat.

'It was an ordinary dream,' the crow begins.

You want to reply, but now that you have an aching urge to talk, the words won't come out.

'It had a sense of unease and longing,' the crow continues, 'but it also had hope and truth. Yes, a very ordinary dream indeed.'

The chair begins to move, and you tighten your grip on the bar as darkness closes in.

The crow's voice, now inside your head, whispers, 'Except for the fact you weren't asleep.'

* * *

[December 2017]

This was a strange experience, and I mean that in a good way. As its title suggests, this story is designed to emulate a dream. Its elements are utterly incoherent at times, but it's all done with intent as it allows the narrative to be constructed entirely in metaphor. The problem is that I'm not sure what any of it means. For every line I decipher, there are two I can't wrap my head around.

Like *Zoia, An Ordinary Dream* heavily fixates on the idea of thoughts and their origin. In this sense, it felt a little repetitive. Sure, it was packaged differently, but it doesn't explore anything new—unless I misunderstood it all. Maybe Warren was going over the same idea because, like me, he had more questions than answers. But for him, I sensed this behaviour would only turn destructive if he didn't move on.

Now, if I imagine myself reading this story without having read any of the others, I enjoy it a lot more. Warren continued to challenge himself with new ways of telling a story, all while constantly provoking thought. However, if you establish yourself as a recognisable writer, the demand for originality is higher. A lot higher. Creating something completely original is difficult because readers can sense when they're experiencing something familiar. This sounds overly critical considering that Warren was still very new to writing, but I think these habits are best kept in check early on so that you're better off in the long run.

The narrator in this story addresses the reader as though they're sitting in that chair looking up at that tree, but this isn't the only way of looking at it. If you look at it from the writer's perspective, placing Warren in that chair, it's like he's stuck inside his own head with a tree of heavy thoughts weighing on his mind.

This was the earliest sign I can remember of Warren struggling with the weight of his ideas, but at least he used this struggle to his advantage and moulded it into a captivating story.

I sent Warren the feedback. I wasn't nearly as critical in the email as I'm being here, but it was still constructive. I thought I was doing the right thing at the time, but now I'm not so sure.

JANUARY 2018

I finally decided to tell Warren what I had been doing for him over the last couple of months. I explained how I shared *Zoia* with a few people I trusted and that I'd love to go over their feedback with him, but before I got a reply, Warren uploaded the second part of *The Unexamined Life*.

The Unexamined Life
Part II: Practice Makes Perfect

Having spoken with The Counsellor, Jimmy leaves The Viewing Room and steps into a clinic corridor.

'Doctor Jimmy!' a voice cheers as the door slams behind him.

A receptionist rushes up to him with a clipboard clutched to her chest. She seems a little too enthusiastic for Jimmy's liking, and, to make matters worse, the pen on top of her ear looks very unstable.

'Your five o'clock is waiting in your office,' she says, bouncing on her toes.

Jimmy stares at the pen on her ear, watching it teeter near its tipping point. 'Where is my office?' he asks.

'You just walked out of it,' she says with a smirk.

Jimmy looks over his shoulder and notices the sign on the door that reads, "Doctor Jimmy". 'Right, I'll just get right back to work then.'

'If you need any help, there's a government-issued script on the table.'

'Do I have one of those scopes?' Jimmy asks.

'A stethoscope? Of course you do! It's on your desk.'

Jimmy turns around with a smile and enters his office. Near the desk at the bottom of the narrow room, a balding middle-aged man rocks back and forth in a chair while aggressively scratching his arm. He doesn't notice Jimmy entering, but the slam of the door forces him to his feet with a gasp.

PART II: PRACTICE MAKES PERFECT

'No need to get up on my account,' Jimmy says.

The patient holds his chest as he catches his breath. 'Please tell me some good news, Jimmy,' he pants.

'Global terrorism is on the decline.'

'What?'

'Yep, we're finally back down to red alert.'

The patient sits back down, wincing in discomfort. 'About my condition, I meant.'

Jimmy sits behind the desk and looks at the patient's arm, noticing blood seeping from scratches across blotchy skin, and he says, 'It doesn't look too good from here, buddy.'

The patient reaches up to his hair and brushes his fingertips across his patchy scalp. All hope drains from his face, and he quietly says, 'Oh God.'

'You were talking about your hair loss?'

'Yes, of course. Why?' The patient realises Jimmy is staring at the rash on his arm. 'You think I should be worrying more about this? You think it's terminal? Like my hair?'

'Calm down, just give me one second.' Jimmy sits forward and examines the notebook on his desk. 'Right, I've got all the results here, and the good news is that there's a process to follow.'

'And what's that?'

'Okay, so we can prescribe you a medication that will recover the loss of some of your hair. Potentially.'

'That's great news, thank y—'

'I'm not finished,' Jimmy cuts in. 'There are some possible side effects, but only minor ones like vomiting, diarrhoea, blood in your stool, and heart palpitations. The only concerning one is—'

'How am I—'

'Please don't interrupt, sir. These guidelines strictly insist I don't let you talk over me. It's all in highlighted capital letters and even underlined. You can't argue with that. Anyway, the main symptom to worry about is the insomnia, as lack of sleep can be a leading cause of hair loss in older men—'

'I'm middle-aged.'

Jimmy turns the notebook around and points at the underlined warning about interruptions. The patient presses his lips together.

'To combat the insomnia,' Jimmy continues, 'I'm going to prescribe another medication, but this one will only have to be taken once a day with food and plenty of water. Oh, I should also mention the hair loss medication has to be taken once every hour, so you'll get five bottles of the stuff to keep you going. The timing is crucial with those. The insomnia medication, however, can be taken whenever you please, but it is a suppository. I know it will be a little awkward, especially with the likelihood of extreme diarrhoea, but I'm sure it'll work if you tilt the right way. Okay, I'll quickly pause for one question only.'

The patient stares.

'It does say here you might need a moment to process all this,' Jimmy goes on, 'so I'll keep talking while you do that to save me some time. Anyway, the insomnia medication does come with its own side effects, but they're mostly the same as the minor side effects of the hair loss medication, so it'll just make those twice as likely to occur. Actually, I read that wrong. It's three times as likely. Not sure why that is, but it's written right here.' Jimmy looks up and smiles.

'Is that everything?' the patient asks.

'We still have to discuss paperwork,' Jimmy replies, going back to the notebook and turning the page. 'We have a few things for you to sign that will protect us if our treatment results in any loss of life—or anything worse, God forbid.' Jimmy starts laughing, but it quickly fades when he looks up and realises the patient didn't get the joke.

'Anyway,' Jimmy continues, shaking his head, 'once we have all that sorted, we can set up a payment plan for you. We have a very low APR of sixty-six point nine per cent, but failure to pay as a result of death requires some sort of family that can make the payments for you, and don't worry if they can't—a lawsuit will sort that out. I can see here you have an extensive family, so that shouldn't be a problem. To apply, we need a blood sample—an additional one to the last several we took—and then we'll do a soft credit check, which shouldn't take more than a month, pending investigation. I can now take two... no, one more question.'

'I think I'll just shave my head,' the patient responds.

'The guide does say you'll probably say that, in which case you can pay off your current bill today, and I'll see you again when that rash gets worse.'

'You think the rash will get worse? Will it be serious?'

'We'll have to run some tests to be sure.'

'I need to be sure. I can't let anything happen to me because my wife is out of work due to illness.'

Jimmy feigns sympathy with a slow nod. 'I'll send off the order later today. You'll get a call to book an appointment with my receptionist so she can fill in a document for a request form. Once the hospital receives the document, they'll send you the request form to fill out. Once that form is returned, they'll let you know a time slot for your pre-test test, where they'll make sure you're fit enough to undergo the required tests for your particular ailment. Sound good?'

'This is all making me feel... '

'Depressed,' Jimmy says with some more nodding and his best attempt to convey empathy with his eyes.

'Yes, I guess that's it,' the patient replies, sinking into a deeper hunch.

'The guide says it's common to feel that way. It's going around a lot and is quite contagious. But I'll set you up with some experimental medication to keep that brain of yours from reacting appropriately to your circumstances.'

'Is that... healthy? Shouldn't I focus on dealing with the issues making me feel this way?'

'Who's the Doctor here?'

'You're right. I'm sorry for questioning your advice.'

'Scepticism will only worsen your conditions.' Jimmy picks up a pen and begins writing up a prescription. 'Now, instructions will be on the bottle, and if it's not too much trouble, please record any side effects you experience. We haven't really been able to test it on anyone yet, so you'll doing us a big favour here. You can sign all the legal documents at the pharmacy.'

The patient takes the prescription and slowly gets up while clutching his chest and grunting in pain. 'Thanks, Doc,' he says, and then he slowly limps out of the room with heavy breaths.

'Can't save them all, Jimmy,' Jimmy tells himself.

The telephone on the desk starts ringing.

'Hello?' Jimmy answers.

'How are you settling in?' The Counsellor replies.

'Not bad. The instructions are easy to follow... '

'But?'

'But this isn't really what I had in mind.'

'General practitioner is a very noble career.'

'I know,' Jimmy says, lowering his head.

'You want to be saving lives that are on the brink of death with only seconds to spare, don't you?'

'Something like that.'

'That kind of work needs a bit more time and practice to build up to. It's not something a guide or script could help you with. Besides, do you really want to be surrounded day in and out by suffering? Like you said, you can't save them all. That kind of sentiment would have a little more significance in intensive care units. Need I remind you that you don't deal well with loss?'

'No,' Jimmy says with a sigh. 'You're right. This was a mistake. Now that you mention it, I don't think I'm really qualified to be a doctor. I hate reading.'

'Shall we talk other options? I've had a few ideas since you

PART II: PRACTICE MAKES PERFECT

left.'

Jimmy takes in a breath and—

'Great!' The Counsellor bursts out. 'So, I've been doing some thinking, and I believe local law enforcement is right up your street—literally just around the corner from where you used to live. You'll get a tailored uniform, too. You're going to love it. I have all the measurements, don't worry. I'm sure you'll also enjoy the job role itself.'

'I don't really know much about the law.'

'Don't worry, I'll partner you up with someone trained in accordance with an official guidebook.'

'Alright then,' Jimmy says in a low voice.

* * *

[January 2018]

This second entry has a very different feel to it compared to the first, as there's far less subtlety but a lot more humour. It's effectively a dark comedy, which is a sudden switch from what started as a meta piece of fiction. This would be jarring if both parts were read in one sitting, but I think the change was Warren's intention.

It makes sense if you think about it within the context of the story. In the beginning, Jimmy's unsure in his every action and comes across as a man with an empty heart, but after he restarts his life, it doesn't seem like he has a heart at all. This is because he not only throws away his old life but also undoes all his development as a husband and father, illustrating how we're moulded by the life we choose to live. It's the only logical explanation.

If anyone else had written such inconsistency, I'd put it down to sloppiness, given the time between writing each part, but because Warren told me he had an ending in mind, I was willing to bet that this sense of disconnect was deliberate. He probably even had it all figured out before the first part. I didn't share these thoughts with Warren at the time because I didn't want to influence his thinking before he got to finish the story.

The biggest thing that stood out for me was the advice given to the patient. It made the scene feel more dystopian than modern, and after the dreamlike nature of *Part I*, it's a suitable fit for the story as a whole because it gives the narrative some sort of progression. But, unlike the switch in personality, I don't think Warren intended this to feel dystopian. He clearly has a strong opinion on clinical treatment, which comes across as personal. *A Tale of Two Pronouns* and *Relatable Jeff* carried this same weight. We all have experiences that shape our work in some way, but the form Warren's stories were taking could only mean he was going through some tough times. It appeared to be taking a toll on his mental health, but I didn't want to assume too much, so I kept this thought to myself for the time being.

I delayed sending my feedback to Warren because I was still waiting for a direct response to the email I sent regarding the endorsements of *Zoia*. I waited a week, constantly checking to make sure I had sent the email to the correct address, but no reply came. I thought the added pressure might have scared him off, but I was only trying to ease any concern or anxiety that comes with being a new writer. I eventually gave in and sent my feedback for *Part II* and hoped Warren had at least read my last email, even if he didn't want to respond.

It took a little while, but I realised my mistake. I was bringing up all these variables to becoming a published author before he'd fully developed his craft. I was too caught up in his stories to realise that he might not view them as I do and would second guess himself like most young writers. I knew I got it wrong, so I decided to cool things off.

I sent him another email apologising for trying to rush him and his work, and he responded in the form of a new story. I was disappointed not to get a direct reply, but given that this was a record-breaking second upload within a single month, I assumed he was focusing solely on his writing rather than letting himself get distracted. Nevertheless, I happily moved on to the next story.

[APPLAUSE]

The three of them stared at the contestant, their lights blinking every few seconds.

I wonder what they'll think about that. The audience had a very mild reaction. Not very telling at all.

'Well, that was interesting,' said the first judge.

This judge always had to get the first word in, and it was always something ambiguous to cause a stir.

Not sure what to make of that, and by the look on their faces, neither does the audience.

The second judge tapped its fingers on the table. 'If I'm honest, that wasn't what I was hoping for, darling.'

It called everyone darling.

That got a murmur going. This doesn't look good.

The third and final judge held its stare the longest. It did this every so often to build tension. A sign lit up in front of the audience and instructed them to hold their breath.

The entire crowd is holding their breath. I think I'd be doing the same if I didn't have to do this voice-over.

'I just can't be bothered to give an opinion on that,' the third judge finally said. 'It was that bad.'

Gasps broke out among the crowd.

Those gasps were the loudest the audience have been all night.

The third judge was always like this. It was known for being harsh, and even if it did have any positive feedback to give, it would be paired with a backhanded comment and

[APPLAUSE]

delivered like a eulogy.

This judge could sing happy birthday to its own mother and make it sound like a death threat.

The contestant was frozen. She didn't know what to say, and even if she did, the words would've been trapped by the lump in her throat.

She doesn't know what to do. This moment will plague her dreams for the next decade. It's safe to say her life has changed for the worse due to one shoddy performance.

The third judge waved its hand, and two silhouettes burst onto the stage and guided the contestant away.

I think the next performer, Zach, will be twice as nervous now. He's been watching the show on the monitors backstage, and we're about to hear his reaction.

The monitor above the stage lit up, and Zach appeared on the screen. He was a timid young man with no noteworthy features beyond the heavy pair of glasses that took up most of his face. He looked a bit peaky, but the intense spotlight above him wasn't doing him any favours.

An arm emerged from the dark and held up a microphone.

'So how confident are you feeling after what you just witnessed?' a voice boomed from nearby speakers.

'I'm not sure,' Zach replied, rapidly blinking. 'I guess I'm as confident as she was before she went out there.'

'So not very confident?'

'I guess not then.'

'Say it then—we need the clip.'

'Say what?'

'That you're not feeling very confident.'

Zach looked beyond the camera, searching for direction.

'Just say it,' the speaker ordered.

'I'm not feeling very confident,' Zach woodenly recited.

'That'll do, head to the marker at the side of the stage and wait for your queue.'

The screen went black.

88

I don't know about you, but he doesn't seem very confident to me. Let's see what the judges make of him.

The lights bulging from the heads of the judges all lit up and pointed at Zach as soon as he stepped from behind the curtain.

He's sweating just from their gaze.

A sign lit up and prompted a mild clap from the audience.

A mild reception, the audience must be a little deflated from the last judging.

Zach stopped in the centre of the stage and removed the microphone from its stand.

'Zach, isn't it, darling?' the second judge asked.

'Yeah, I—'

'What will you be performing for us today?' the third judge interrupted.

Zach swallowed and said, 'I'll be writing—'

'You'll be writing what?'

'A book about—'

'A book about what?'

Zach wiped the sweat from his forehead. 'Memories.'

'Fictional?'

Zach took a moment to think about it.

'Yes or no?' The third judge pressed.

'Yes and no,' Zach answered, just barely.

The judges look a little confused—not the best first impression.

'How's that then?' the first judge asked, gesturing for Zach to raise the microphone.

Zach held the microphone closer to his mouth and said, 'Memories are... I guess, similar to dreams when you're—'

'Sounds good,' the third judge interrupted. 'Take a seat at your desk and begin.'

A sign instructed the crowd to clap, but not too encouragingly.

Even the crowd seems a little hesitant about this idea.

[APPLAUSE]

Several stagehands stormed into the spotlight and placed a typewriter, desk, and stool in the centre of the stage. Zach set the microphone down on the desk and sat on the stool. The spotlight dimmed, allowing Zach a look at the nondescript faces in the audience, and every one of them met his eye with a blank stare.

He's ready.

Zach brought his fingers to the typewriter, and a sign prompted the audience to lean forward, which they all did as one. Zach's attention was momentarily drawn towards the synchronised display of nail-biting tension. Before he could even look down, his fingers were already at work, albeit rather slowly. He usually typed a lot faster, but he was scared of making a mistake in front of hundreds of people.

He's not a speedy typist, but that's owed to his meticulous choice of words, much like a poet weaving the perfect rhyme. Well, that's what his parents put on the application form.

A sign instructed some of the audience to sit back.

A few members of the crowd aren't taking to Zach's performance at this early stage, but maybe they'll be convinced before the end.

Zach's head started to ache as his fingers grew tired. He cracked his knuckles and kept going, but his forearms were getting tighter by the minute. The heat of the spotlight only added to the distress, though it didn't burn half as much as the crowd's unblinking gaze. He could push through the physical pain, but mentally, he was crumbling. The words on the page started to fade, and a sign prompted some murmuring.

The crowd is getting agitated. They were expecting more from this contestant.

Zach hit the keys harder, trying to force the words out, but it was no use; the ink was drying up before his eyes. His hands slid from the keys and fell to his lap, and the crowd was commanded to gasp. Zach couldn't bear to look anyone in the eye, so he kept his head down.

This isn't good.
He's going to let down a lot of people.

Some of the audience clapped in encouragement, but a sign lit up and prompted silence.

Looks like we'll have to wait this one out.

The judges were disinterested, much like everyone else who was watching. At this point, it wouldn't make a difference to them if Zach started writing again or not.

It's been a little over six months. Surely he'll start again sometime soon. He's only got himself to let down now because everybody else has given up.

Zach's eyes were fixed on the paper sticking out of the typewriter. He knew what he wanted to write but didn't know how to get started again. Does he just trust his fingers and not think about it? What if he gets it wrong? What if he makes a mistake? He'd want to start all over again, but that's not something they'll accept. Maybe more time will help.

There's some movement. Zach has finally raised his arms.

The crowd was prompted to lean forward.

Oh, he's just resting his elbows on the desk. God forbid he gets uncomfortable while we sit here waiting.

The crowd, unprompted, leaned back and collectively sighed.

Zach had stopped giving himself excuses not to write. He just didn't want to anymore. He wondered what was in it for him. Was it just about the story he wanted to tell? Would it even matter if it was told? It wouldn't make a difference to anyone. But... that wasn't the point. That's not the reason he started writing in the first place. He started because he needed somewhere to record his ideas so that his mind would have room to breathe, and there was a passion for stories and the art of how they're told—in the meaning of providing meaning.

[APPLAUSE]

It was for himself because he was never writing to satisfy strangers. So why couldn't he bear this crowd? Why did they have such a hold on him? Was it the pressure they brought? It felt like a need to be validated, but no matter what he did from here, that feeling would only ever grow. There was no escaping it.

Then I'll just have to embrace it, he told himself. Give them something to judge and crave their validation. They can take everything, but don't let them take away your passion. Fall in love with the story first, and indulge in the worst parts of yourself later.

Zach sat straight and furrowed his brows.

Movement at last, but will it mean anything? Will it even matter fifteen months after he started?

A sign prompted the crowd into a nail-biting position. The judges sprang forward as Zach placed his fingers on the keys.

Is this it?

Zach began writing faster than ever before. Thoughts and ideas that had been bottled and left to mature for months were now being poured onto the page.

This is what everyone came to see. Will he be able to finish it this time?

It was tiring, but the want to finish was greater than the need to rest, so he kept going. There was a mix of anxiety and excitement in the crowd, and not one of them could look away.

A couple of weeks had passed, yet the audience was as keen as ever. They watched every one of Zach's sore fingers as they mashed the keys with confidence. Their anticipation provided crucial mental support for Zach, who was just about holding on.

Suddenly, there was silence, and everyone in the auditorium held their breath. The endless tapping of keys had comforted them, but now their ears were troubled with an insistent inch to hear something—anything, really.

Zach threw his hands in the air and smiled wider than he ever had before. He was finished. The crowd sighed with relief, and one or two were even allowed to clap.

Zach stood up and grabbed the microphone. 'Thank you,' he said half-heartedly.

'Well,' the first judge started, 'we finally got there.'

Zach laughed nervously.

'That was some wait,' the second judge said, 'but... was it worth it?'

The third judge began massaging its head. 'That was disappointing.'

The crowd was ordered to look shocked.

Can't say I'm surprised by that. It was always going to be a tough recovery after the wait.

'I'm not totally blown away by it,' the first judge put in. 'Then again, it's not the worst performance I've seen.'

'I can appreciate that,' Zach replied.

'Your bit is done,' the third judge snapped. 'You don't do anything from here, so just stand there and show some basic emotions that can easily be described.'

Zach put down the microphone and tucked his hands into his pockets.

'You know, overall, I actually really enjoyed it,' the second judge said. 'It wasn't the best I've seen, but at least it was a little different.'

'I don't know about different,' the first judge challenged.

'It's nothing new to me,' the third judge added, 'but that doesn't mean I think it was completely terrible. It was just... mostly terrible.'

This is a very mixed response. Nobody can agree.

'I think he deserves some credit for seeing it through,' the second judge offered.

'That is the minimum we expect,' the third judge replied. 'We don't praise people just for completing what they already promised they'd complete. We're strictly judging the performance itself.'

'So what does it matter if the performance was staggered then?' the second judge countered. 'If we ignore the delay and focus on the substance of the performance, can you really say it was that bad?'

The third judge sat back and crossed its arms. 'Yes I can, and yes I am.'

'I do see your point,' the first judge said, looking at the second judge, 'but I can see why someone wouldn't enjoy it. Overall, I guess it was... okay. I'm not going to get too caught up in the controversy.'

We're going to have to bring in the judgement judges, something we only do when there's no conclusive decision from the three down in front.

A spotlight directed attention to the second-level balcony where the judgement judges were seated, and a boom microphone settled above them as their lights lit up.

They are quite intimidating, aren't they?

'Very different opinions,' the first judgement judge began. 'I think the third judge is notorious for its harsh judgement, and most of the time, it's just trying to keep up the character.'

'Character?' the third judge roared.

'You've had your say,' the first judgement judge replied.

The third judge sprang to its feet and yelled, 'Well, I'm having my say on this!'

'You don't judge the judgement judges judging. That would be utterly ridiculous—we have judgement judge reviewers for that, so let me finish, please.'

The third judge sat down and folded its arms.

It doesn't look pleased, does it?

'Anyway,' the first judgement judge continued, 'the second judge doesn't really seem to have any standards, so just about anything can get a lukewarm approval from it.'

The second judge looks ready for a fight after that comment.

'And then there's the first judge, who doesn't really have the correct programming to judge a performance like this. It's going to get cold up there on the fence sooner or later.'

Oh dear, that must have hit a nerve.

The first judge can't keep still in its seat right now.

The first judgement judge took a small sip of water and looked to its left, where the second judgement judge was flicking through a small notepad.

'I don't think any of what you just said was genuine,' the second judgement judge finally said, looking to the side.

'Who? Me?' the first judgement judge replied.

'Yes, you.'

'And why is that?'

'I think you're trying to discredit the judges down there because you think you know better than them. Not everything needs to be a critical analysis. It's possible they simply didn't like what they saw, and there doesn't have to be a motive or reason behind it. All we're here to do is get a decisive opinion out of them.'

'Thank you,' the third judge said, flailing its arms.

It looks thankful for that comment.

'That's pretty much what I was going to say,' the third judgement judge put in. 'Based on what the three down there said, I think this performance has a select audience, but it probably wouldn't wow them. I think that's perfectly valid.'

'Great, you're teaming up against me,' the first judgement judge said.

'See, there it is again,' the third judgement judge replied. 'Everything to you is driven by some motive. Just listen to what's being said and stop conspiring as to why it's being said. Do you think it's possible that you're the critic with a motive, not them?'

'How? I'm calling it all out. It's why we're here.'

'And there you go,' the second judgement judge interjected. 'You're trying to find controversy, but you're only coming across

[APPLAUSE]

as hypocritical.'

'I'm not having this.' The first judgement judge got out of its seat and marched out of the light.

It bailed pretty quickly, didn't it?

Well, it's up to the two remaining judgement judges to make a decision here.

'Right,' the second judgement judge continued, 'I don't think there's much to look into here. That's not to say it's completely fair. I do agree that the first judge is being too safe in its feedback, but that's more of a testament to the lacking performance.'

The third judgement judge nodded in agreement and said, 'Performances that get through don't put people on the fence, there should be no doubt involved, and those standards are important for the show.'

'Standards?' the first judgement judge shouted from the shadows. 'Ha!'

That concludes the judgement of the judgement judges. We can finally go back to the judges.

'Sorry, Zach,' the third judge said, 'you're not making it through. But I think we can all agree that you should keep at it because there's potential in you, so don't throw it away.'

'Yes,' the first and second judges said together.

Zach snatched up the microphone. 'To be honest, I didn't come here expecting to be the next best thing. I just wanted to share what I do with—'

The microphone cut out and left Zach talking to himself on stage. He tried shouting his words, but a sign prompted a burst of applause from the audience, drowning out every word he said.

* * *

[January 2018]

This story steps away from the world of dreams and dystopian politics and gets closer to the surreal. This was obviously written as a response to my advice on getting stories in front of people, but it reveals a lot more than I realised during my first read.

The narrative is driven by anxiety—by the thought of putting yourself in front of people and not knowing what will happen. This could've been a simple ironic twist of the talent show format, given that they only exist for performance-based talent, but this story gets increasingly more absurd to get its point across. What is that point, though? It's very unclear at first, and it seems like a general attack on reality TV, but that's too literal. It's never that simple. I think the stage is used to create a rendition of thought and emotion, especially in relation to them being affected by the people around you. And that's just what's on the surface of this story.

You might have noticed that the judges aren't human. I'm not sure what they are, but I can only assume they're machines because they have blinking lights. What I think Warren is getting at here is an idea that people often respond according to expectations, like they're preprogrammed. This same idea is shown through an audience that's prompted when and how to react, which is supported by a voice-over that relays redundant information. It suggests that if there are no original creations, there are no authentic reactions, which renders criticism meaningless.

On top of all this, there are judges for the judges. Now, the naming of these characters causes a messy read in places, but as usual, Warren finds a way to make it purposeful for the type of narrative he's exploring. His unusual approach to technique doesn't always work, but here it adds to the surreality of the story.

Anyway, these so-called judgement judges don't have any preconfigured responses, and when one calls out a judge for being too harsh, it's quickly shut down and told that sometimes people just don't like things. This is either a commentary on the treatment of different opinions or a basic notion that criticism itself doesn't suggest ulterior motives, so if we can't accept the latter, we should stay off the stage. None of this is a revelation, but alongside the other elements of the story, it shows the kind of worries going through Warren's mind. Maybe that's why he didn't reply in an email. Anxiety isn't something you can easily explain, so why not use a story to convey it instead?

I think it comes down to one important line:

"The judges were disinterested, much like everyone else who was watching. At this point, it wouldn't make a difference to them if Zach started writing again or not."

For all the answers Warren gave me with this story, he left behind one question for himself, and it was one of motivation. As you should know by now, Warren likes to take his time when writing; that's just his process, and that's fine. But when you look ahead, beyond all that time yet to pass, you might ask yourself, is there anyone left? Would anyone really wait for you? Why would they? It's a daunting thought for many, and it's not irrational. In my experience, if you want to make something of yourself, you have to be consistently constant and constantly consistent. At what point do you compromise your work to please everyone but yourself?

This story was a turning point. Warren was consumed with these recurring ideas of thought and criticism, and his concepts started down a darker path. It wasn't affecting the quality of his stories, but it did change how he approached them. You'll see what I mean.

I decided to give Warren a call after reading *[APPLAUSE]*. I honestly didn't think he would answer, but surprisingly he did. He wasn't as keen to talk about writing as he had been in the past. I encouraged him to get back to stories like *Zoia* and not focus on these bleak narratives with introspective themes because it would only drag him down.

'Drag me down how?' he asked.

'Mentally. If you're focused on critical analysis of your work as you write it, you'll start questioning yourself to the point where you'll change the most minute aspects of your stories until they're absolutely perfect.'

'Didn't you tell me already that no story is perfect?' he replied.

'Yes, that's the point. You can't write something impervious to criticism, so you'll hit a wall sooner or later if you keep going in this direction.'

'It's fine. I'll go around the wall.'

See what I had to put with? He would say anything to avoid an answer.

'Why build it in the first place if it's just going to get in your way?' I asked.

'I guess I like a challenge.'

'Is that thought one of your own?' I replied, thinking I was being clever without considering that he'd be prepared for a question like that.

'If it isn't, I wouldn't be obliged to answer, would I?' he countered.

'And if it is?'

'That's irrelevant if you don't know the answer to your first question.'

I fell silent. I clearly didn't know him as well as I thought.

'Did you get my email about *Zoia*?' I asked, changing the subject.

'Yes,' he replied in a way that suggested he didn't want to continue the conversation.

'And?' I pressed.

'I know what you're trying to do, and I appreciate the support, but I'm not at that point yet.'

'I'm just showing you that there's an audience for your writing, that's all.'

He either sighed or huffed, I couldn't tell, and then he said, 'I get that, but I don't want to think about others and what they have to think about me. Not at the moment, anyway.'

'Alright, I understand,' I replied, not fully understanding.

I knew that he didn't want to be pressured, and I was trying to be more patient with him, but what was wrong with discussing the positive response his story received? It was confusing. I told him I was looking forward to his next upload, and we ended the call.

FEBRUARY 2018

I kept thinking about that phone call throughout February. I was slightly annoyed with Warren, but I was far more annoyed with myself. I knew I had missed something, so I reread every story hoping to find some answers, but all I found were the same questions. I was going in circles. Even with all those words staring back at me, I couldn't read between the lines. It was infuriating, almost like Warren was taunting me indirectly. At this point, it was clear I needed to take a step back from reading, but when Warren uploaded a new story at the end of the month, I didn't even try to resist.

Silhouettes and Epithets

The halogen bulb flickered as though it was holding on for dear life. Three subjects entered the room with their eyes fixed on the floor, and each of them sat down in an empty chair, all lined up in a row facing a double layer of transparent polycarbonate sheet.

This opening line is a little too dramatic for a light bulb description. Do we need to know that it's halogen? A bulb is a bulb. And why not just say window? Are you showing off a degree in plastics? Why even specify it's double glazing? It's not an important detail. And if their eyes were fixed on the floor, how come they didn't trip over the chairs? At what point did they look up? Also, if someone is going to sit in a chair, we assume they're not about to sit on someone's lap, so you don't need to tell us the chairs are empty. It's useless information.

They all spotted a silhouette facing them on the other side of the plastic. They leaned forward together, and the darkness began to lift.

How do they know it's facing them if it's a silhouette?

The first of these three subjects was Laura. She squinted and the shade lifted from the stranger before her, revealing long brunette hair paired with sunken grey eyes.

Are the eyes in her hair? All this is far too confusing for an introduction.

'Look at you, String Bean,' Laura said to the stranger. 'You should eat more.'

The stranger lowered her head and forced a smile on one side of her face.

Which side? This isn't clear enough.

The man next to Laura, Max, also started to see the stranger's features, but he saw something else entirely. He saw dry red hair and scarred skin riddled with acne.

'I don't know you, Spotty, and I already don't like you,' Max said. 'I don't want to get too close. You look contagious.'

The stranger turned away.

This guy isn't likeable enough. I hope he's not the main character. Who even is the protagonist?

The final subject, Abigail, saw that the stranger's face was so bloated it concealed any evidence of bone structure.

'You need to lose some weight, Piggy,' Abigail said. 'A lot of weight, actually.'

The stranger covered her face with her hands and started to sob.

Am I supposed to enjoy this? All of this is horrible. How many people will feel upset after reading this? I'm sorry, I'm not reading any further. What a waste of time.

Laura looked at Max and didn't think he was contagious. She only saw his bright blue eyes, complimented by a kind smile and full cheeks.

Max had noticed her staring at him from the corner of his

eye. He thought she was intimidated by him, maybe even scared.

It was always the pretty ones, he thought. The ones with soft, glowing skin and vibrant hair.

Abigail saw them both looking at each other. She was used to being the forgotten one in the room. Why on earth would someone with that body want to eat more, she thought, looking at Laura. Imagine having a body that allowed you to wear whatever you wanted, where you could show off some skin without people laughing at you.

Laura spotted Abigail looking at her, and Abigail quickly looked away. She probably thinks I'm starving myself, Laura thought, looking down at her waist and wishing she had worn something more concealing. She was tired of looking as ill as people often told her and dreamed of having curves like Abigail. At that moment, she felt more vulnerable than ever.

Abigail had turned her attention to Max. She thought he looked kind and approachable, and that he'd have no trouble fitting in and finding friends. She had always wondered what that would be like.

Max looked to the other corner of his eye, fearing Abigail was staring at his blotchy neck or dry scalp. It's okay for her, he thought. She doesn't have to worry about people glaring at her face. She doesn't even need make-up. How amazing it must feel to have such a natural beauty and be so comfortable in your own skin.

They all looked back at the stranger but only saw a window into the next room. For a moment, they stared, and then they stood up and stared some more.

Not a word was exchanged between any of them as they left the room one at a time.

* * *

[February 2018]

Warren had gone in the opposite direction of my advice and embraced everything I told him not to. I would've been annoyed if not for the positive message of the story, despite it starting with much of what I expected. At least he clearly laid out what he wanted to say and left little ambiguity. It's the kind of story that needs to be concise with its message, so he did that part very well. The problem is that he had more to say about criticism, which was starting to get tedious. He does at least use the theme differently this time, as it highlights the value of patience instead of reiterating the same points as *[APPLAUSE]*.

The reviewer at the beginning of the story, which I didn't fully grasp at first, doesn't want to give the writer a chance and makes too many assumptions before getting to the story's underlying message. Then the reviewer stops reading, labelling it offensive and a waste of time. Warren has a valid point here. Some people hold certain expectations when reading something out of their comfort zone and set themselves up to be disappointed. I was guilty of this myself a few years ago. It's an easy trap to fall into. When you take a risk in reading a book that confuses you at first, even by design, the safer bet is to not gamble any more time and use it elsewhere instead. After all, if you quit before you're ahead, you won't know what you've missed. Whether that's good or bad, I can't say.

The second side of this story is about how we see ourselves compared to how others see us, and it highlights how we ignore each other in that process. It made me question myself for a moment. In my head, I pictured myself in that chair and contemplated what I'd think if I saw myself as a stranger looking back at me. It's quite meditative, depending on your ability to concentrate, but I couldn't focus on the worst of myself like the characters in the story, so I put Warren in the chair next to me and found myself more concerned about his thoughts as he stared at himself. He must share some of the emotions this story evokes because, much like the characters, he never talked openly about his feelings. If only I knew what was holding him back.

This narrative made me wonder what Warren valued in others and what would be enough to make him envious. People have an imperfect way of looking at themselves, so maybe it would be something to do with his work, as he certainly didn't see his stories the way I did. Perhaps his struggles came from comparing his writing ability to other writers he knew, making him question if he would ever live up to their standards.

In all my efforts to help Warren see the value of his writing, I was never able to protect him from himself. I felt like I was losing the battle at this point. I had no idea what to do to help him find new inspiration, and it wouldn't have mattered anyway because he was no longer replying to my emails or returning my calls. I just had to wait and hope he would eventually talk to me again.

MAY 2018

I had kept myself occupied during the last few weeks by editing some of Warren's stories to eliminate typos and grammatical errors. It wasn't my speciality, but it was a way to help Warren while he isolated himself. I also continued introducing his stories to more writers, bloggers, and everyday readers. I wanted to find his audience because it would help him focus on consistent themes that were free from fixation and anxiety. He'd then know how to market his stories, which were all connecting with a broader demographic than I'd hoped, but it was better than no data at all.

Warren finally responded to me a few days into May, and as I'd anticipated, it was via another upload. This one got me quite excited when I saw the title.

The Unexamined Life
Part III: Job 10:10

The police station has a very different odour compared to the clinic. There's a lot more vinegar in the air.

'You're the new boy then,' a voice said.

Jimmy turns to face an approaching constable who's wearing every possible layer of uniform and snacking on salt and vinegar crisps. It isn't exactly what Jimmy expected, but it doesn't surprise him either.

'I assume I am,' Jimmy responds.

'Why haven't you got your gear on?' the officer asks.

'Because... I don't know where it is?'

'It's in the locker room.'

'And where's that?'

'You just walked out of it.'

Jimmy looks over his shoulder. 'Ah, "locker room", of course.'

'Get your stuff together and meet me out front in the car. I'm Mark, by the way.'

'Do I get my own locker?'

'First one on your right as you go in—keys are in the lock. You have ten minutes, newbie.'

Jimmy smiles with excitement.

'You don't need to wear the hat in the car,' Mark says as Jimmy climbs in.

'Noted,' Jimmy replies, lifting the hat off his head and

placing it neatly on his lap.

Static erupts from the handheld radio on the dashboard. 'Units respond. We have a ten-forty-five on Briers Street, south of the city centre.'

'What's that mean?' Jimmy asks.

'It means we ignore it,' Mark laughs.

'But someone might need help.'

'You can't help them all, newbie.'

Jimmy's eyes narrow. 'How did you become a policeman?'

'Sort of just happened, I guess.'

'How can it just sort of happen?'

'How did you become a policeman?' Mark counters.

'Well... sort of just happened.'

'Funny that.'

The radio comes alive again. 'Units respond. We have a ten-ten at Saint Nicolas' church.'

'That's a good one,' Mark beamed, turning the engine on.

'What's a ten-ten?' Jimmy asks.

'Inebriated person.'

'How did you memorise all these numbers?'

Mark removes a small book from his pocket. 'Just keep reading this government guidebook until it sinks in,' he says, tossing the book over to Jimmy. 'Simple as that. Also helps that I've been a ten-ten on many occasions.' Mark breaks into a laugh, but it quickly fizzles out when he catches Jimmy's vacant stare.

Jimmy opens the guidebook, holding it by his fingertips, and brings it to the end of his nose. 'How am I supposed to read writing this small?'

Mark breaks into a laugh once again and picks up the radio. 'Car two-one-two here. Ten-four, chill your beans.'

'What does that mean?' Jimmy asks, looking over the top of the guidebook.

'It's like... calm your tits, but classier.'

'I meant the ten-four.'

PART III: JOB 10:10

'Doesn't mean a thing, just sounds cool.'

Jimmy eyes slowly drift back to the guidebook.

Mark and Jimmy arrive on the scene, screeching to a stop.

'Jesus,' Jimmy blurts.

'Cut me some slack, newbie. I've not had my license long.'

'No, Jesus,' Jimmy repeats, pointing out a grubby man arguing with a bronze statue of Jesus.

'Oh no, that's Stilton,' Mark says. 'This ain't going to be fun.'

'You've nicknamed him after a cheese? That's demeaning.'

'He gave himself the nickname because he loves the stuff,' Mark replies, fumbling with his seatbelt. 'Mind you, I do enjoy cheese. There's also Feta, Cheddar, Brie—'

'You don't have to list every type of cheese,' Jimmy interrupts.

Mark finally unbuckles himself. 'No, that's all his mates.'

'Oh,' Jimmy replies, putting his hat on. 'They sound delightful.'

They get out of the car and approach the suspect.

'You take the lead,' Mark whispers. 'Newbie practice.'

Jimmy exhales nervously as he stops behind the grubby man. 'Stilton, isn't it?'

'Who you calling Stilton?' the man bellows, spinning around. 'You stuck-up twat!'

'That's my bad,' Mark intervenes. 'This is Stuart. I got him confused.'

'Great start,' Jimmy mutters.

Mark pushes his thumbs into his belt and puffs out his chest. 'Okay, Stuart, what you doing?'

'What's it look like I'm doing?' Stuart replies, looking into Jimmy's soul.

'Am I supposed to know?' Jimmy asks, taking a step back.

'Because I have absolutely no clue—you're talking to a statue of Jesus.'

Stuart steps closer. 'Spot on, but who does he report to?'

'God?' Jimmy answers with a shrug.

'Bingo wings! My prayers are falling on dumb drums, so I'm stabbing the messenger.'

Jimmy leans towards Mark and asks, 'Do we just arrest him?'

'Please!' Stuart roars.

'We're not arresting you, Stuart,' Mark snaps. He turns to Jimmy and quietly says, 'He's always doing this. He wants to go to jail so he has a place to sleep. He's trying to cheat the system, but we simply don't have the room for him.'

'You took Gentle Gene!' Stuart yells.

Mark sighs. 'He stabbed a delivery driver for a pizza.'

'Sure it wasn't Mozzarella?' Jimmy says, holding back a grin.

Mark gives him a stern look.

'Is that what it'll take?' Stuart continues. 'I can do that too, and I'm not fussy with toppings.'

Jimmy raises his hand and says, 'Wait, so you're homeless?'

'You think I dress and smell like shit because it's fashionable? Fuck you, you arrogant asshole.'

'Hey, easy, I'm new to this. I think we can put you in overnight, at least. It seems like the safest option here.'

'No!' Mark snaps. 'That isn't happening. It's not how the system works.'

'The system is there to protect people, isn't it? Seems like we'd be helping him and the public by just locking him up for the night.'

'And he'll be doing the same thing tomorrow until we lock him up another night. At that point, he might as well go to prison.'

'Yes!' Stuart cheers. 'Free meals for life!'

Mark folds his arms with clenched fists. 'Absolutely not.'

Jimmy pulls Mark aside. 'Why are you so adamant to keep him out here?' he whispers.

PART III: JOB 10:10

'I'm just following guidelines.'

'And what are those guidelines?'

'He'd just be taking up space. We have limited time and money, and this guy has zero chance of reform.'

'Isn't re-offending rates at an all-time high? Whatever you're trying to do, it's not working.'

'Look, people like him have a low survival rate, so why waste money putting him in prison?'

Jimmy stands straight. 'So you're saying it's more cost-effective to wait until he dies out here?'

'I wouldn't say that, but... the statistics would.'

'I don't really know what to say to that.'

'Now you're getting it, newbie.'

They turn back to Stuart but only find Jesus smiling down at them.

'Shit, he must have gone inside,' Mark says.

'What's wrong with that? I thought everyone was welcome here?'

'I think you missed the small print.'

'In the bible?' Jimmy says. 'It's all small print.'

Mark marches forward. 'Come on, let's go and get him out of there.'

The inside of the church is cold and empty, and the biblical decoration fails to lend any significance to the size of the nave. The Vicar beams towards the officers; his footsteps bounce around the entire room.

'Why can't you people ever do your job properly?' the Vicar scorns. 'I asked he be removed from the premises, and you let him in? Look at what the fool is doing.'

Jimmy looks towards the sound of splashing and finds Stuart bent over a basin of holy water washing his armpits.

'It doesn't take too long to whip up a new batch, though, right?' Jimmy asks, sincerity in his voice.

'It's not like I'm brewing beer in here like some monk,

young man. It's the principle of not desecrating a place of worship.'

'Maybe try speaking to him. This could be his way of asking for help.'

'He doesn't want help,' the Vicar snaps. 'He wants trouble.'

'Is that what you believe or what you tell yourself to make it easier to condemn him?'

Mark steps in between them. 'Whoa there, newbie, let's not get into a debate here.'

'What do you believe in?' the Vicar asks, looking past Mark.

'The highest bidder,' Jimmy answers, pointing and winking, immediately sensing how stupid he must look.

'Not much, then. Seeing is believing, right? That's how you get led astray.'

'You talk like an advert. And if there exists the epitome of the phrase "led astray", it would simply be a picture of you in that get-up. You seem to question everything and everyone except yourself.'

'You don't know me, boy. Don't pretend like you do. I refuse to be generalised based on your own misgivings.'

'You tell him, Elvis,' a voice taunts.

The Vicar turns around to find Stuart seated in the aisle.

'Get up,' the Vicar barks.

'Hold on, will you,' Stuart replies, taking off one of his tattered shoes. 'This one's bugging me, you know. It squeaks in a German accent when I walk. The other one is from china and keeps quiet most of the time, but this one, the atrocities, can you imagine!'

The Vicar looks at the shoe and then back at Stuart. 'What on earth are you going on about?'

'Politics!' Stuart roars. 'You think this shoe is here legally? Like fuck is it! It came over like the rest of them. Look at it! Dodgy bastard.'

He thrusts the shoe up at the Vicar and then brings it to

PART III: JOB 10:10

his eyes. 'Where's your papers?'

'He's insane.' The Vicar slowly backs away. 'I need him out of here right this instant.'

'To be fair to him,' Jimmy interjects, 'at least he's talking to something tangible. You tell your hopes and dreams to an imaginary friend.'

'That's enough from you. Do your job and arrest him.'

Stuart bursts to his feet. 'The king has spoken. Now take me away.'

'We're not going to arrest you!' Mark yells. 'Now come on, you've had your fun.'

Stuart jumps out of Mark's reach. 'You think this is fun for me? Look at you standing there in your tidy uniform. Do you know what you look like in that? I bet you can't even look yourself in the mirror to answer that, can you? I knew a man just like you once. He wore a thimble as a hat and sang hymns to the mice to make the birds jealous. Oh, and jealous they were. They stopped inviting him to parties and told all his friends he used ready-steady-dough in all his pies.'

Mark lunges forward and catches Stuart's arm. 'Grab him, newbie.'

'Don't you see?' Stuart bellows. 'It was about the pies all along!'

Jimmy calmly walks up to Stuart and takes hold of his other arm. 'What do we do with him?'

'We'll pop him in the back of the car and take him into town,' Mark replies. 'He lives around there most of the time.'

'I live everywhere, Captain Kangaroo,' Stuart says, 'and nowhere at the same time.'

Jimmy looks from Mark to Stuart and then back to Mark. 'I don't think we're doing a good thing here.'

'What do you know of good things,' the Vicar says.

'I know what I learnt of right and wrong didn't come from fiction. How would you ever know the difference between an original idea and an idea of someone else's idea?'

The Vicar doesn't bother to reply and marches towards the basin.

'He has loud steps for a man wearing blue suede shoes,' Stuart says with a smirk. 'Do you know who he reports to? Wrong. Nobody knows. He doesn't even know.'

'He'd report to God, wouldn't he?' Jimmy indulges as he barely assists Mark in dragging Stuart towards the door.

'On a scale of one to ten, how much did your last shit look like shit?' Stuart asks.

'Don't answer that, newbie.'

Jimmy holds eye contact with Mark for a moment, and then he turns to Stuart in defiance and says, 'Ten.'

'So you do know shit when you see it, but only when it's coming from your arse and not your mouth. You poor sick man. Have you been diagnosed yet? I can do it right here for free—you're an idiot. On top of that, you've got an image of a shit you took earlier stored in your head. That's beyond troubling. The Freemasons will know what to do. Call them up, but if Jack answers, tell him it's the wrong number.'

Stuart kicks the back of Mark's seat.

'Oi, I'm trying to drive here!' Mark shouts.

'I'm hungry,' Stuart says, rocking back and forth.

'You're annoying.'

'Maybe we should just get him some takeaway,' Jimmy suggests.

'No fucking way!' Stuart yells, kicking the seat again.

'Oi!' Mark shouts, even louder than before.

Stuart sinks into the seat. 'You ain't feeding me crap like that,' he says, crossing his arms. 'The Tesco around the corner will have their bins full at this time of day. Let's go.'

'We're not digging food out of a bin for you,' Mark replies.

Jimmy turns to face Stuart, looking through the barrier at him. 'You'd rather eat trash than takeaway?'

'What kind of question is that? Of course I would. Have

PART III: JOB 10:10

you seen what they use to cook takeaways?'

'Lard? Oil?'

'No, manic depressives. You can taste their sadness in the food. That's why the chips are soggy. You think all that salt and vinegar makes up for it? Wrong. Tomato sauce, maybe, but I hate to play odds like that. I'm not a gambler. Used to be—gambled on a wife, now I'm down two kids and a testicle, but it was rigged, I'm sure of it. You don't get that kind of uncertainty with bins. No matter what, you know you'll get shit food. No risk, all reward.'

Jimmy looks perplexed. 'That isn't... entirely illogical. But I think—'

'You don't think!' Stuart snaps. 'You relay! Like you said to Elvis back there, how would you know the difference between an original idea and an idea of someone else's idea of an original idea? Or something like that. You thinking is just your brain feeding you lines from what you've read or heard, and there's no filter. You prick.'

'There is if you question instead of answer.'

'Where'd you get that one? Sceptics weekly? I'm bored of you. Put the radio on and have a chat with it.'

'I told you not to try having a conversation with him,' Mark says, pulling up outside a chip shop. 'I'll take him in and see what he wants. You hungry?'

'No, I'm good, thanks. You know he said he didn't want takeaway, right?'

'This isn't the first time I've done this. He'll pick something once I get him in there, and then he'll go away.'

'You're paying then, Captain Crunch,' Stuart says, unbuckling his shoes from the seat next to him.

Once Mark and Stuart are inside the chip shop, Jimmy picks up the radio and changes the frequency until he hears white noise.

'I wondered when I'd hear from you,' The Counsellor says.

'It's been an interesting one,' Jimmy replies.

'Is that good or bad?'

'I uh... I don't feel I have freedom here. Being confined to a flawed system means I can't do anything meaningful.'

'Meaningful? I thought you just wanted to help people, Jimmy?'

'That is meaningful.'

'But to who? You or them? What's more important?'

'Both,' Jimmy answers without hesitation.

'Pending intention.'

'But if my inten—'

'Just come back through already,' The Counsellor snaps. 'There's a fire door in the alleyway. Your clothes are in the bin next to it.'

✳ ✳ ✳

[May 2018]

I was glad Warren decided to continue this story. I knew it was planned to be written in parts, that was the fundamental concept, but I was worried that he'd push this aside to continue exploring the same themes as the last two uploads. I think he came back to this to give himself a rest from his other ideas, and I was really excited about it at first, but that quickly changed.

Part III feels more contemporary than the previous part, and to be consistent with its own inconsistency, Jimmy's personality changes yet again. This time he's more grounded and questions everything rather than casually accepting the situation like he did in *Part II*, but instead of just questioning, he's sceptical of everything. This reminds me so much of Warren, and I doubt that's by chance. It's clear that, like the previous entry, this part was inspired by his own experiences, but now he was putting a little of himself into his characters to vent frustration, which means the story is driven by all the wrong reasons.

I started reading *Part III* with the assumption it would be a satire on law enforcement. Even the use of police code in the title suggested this until I realised it was actually from the bible. The verse reads: "Hast thou not poured me out as milk, and curdled me like cheese?" It fits perfectly with the story because religion is called into question more than the law, to the point where Jimmy seems to have a personal grievance against God. It isn't a good look for the character, but I think the dialogue is less about challenging the Vicar's beliefs and more about using his faith as an easy example of the origin of thought.

"How would you know the difference between an original idea and an idea of someone else's idea."

Jimmy's words reflect a common theme Warren uses in

his work, as though he's trying to find one conclusive answer to whether his stories are truly his own creation. *Zoia* encompassed this idea the most, and while it was interesting initially, it was now creating more insecurities for Warren. He was only digging the hole deeper by using Jimmy to directly externalise his own thoughts. He started this story back when he had more clarity, and instead of rediscovering that sense, he realised just how unclear his mind had become.

I tried to warn him about this. Warren was now writing for himself and treating it like a hobby rather than a profession. It begs the question of why he bothered to share his work with me at all. My attempts to get to know him only revealed how little I could ever understand him.

JUNE 2018

Warren's next upload came in the form of a poem. His notebook had rough drafts of poetic verses but nothing close to complete. This was his first poem that had structure and purpose, although I didn't quite understand why it took him over three weeks to produce something that should only take a couple of hours at most. I began to wonder what might be filling up his time. Was he focusing more on his animation work? Or perhaps, as this next story suggests, he was spending most of his time staring at a blank page, hoping words would form by themselves. I know that feeling all too well.

The kneading of a want.

Sometimes it's difficult to find the right words.
   You can ponder for days and still not ease the struggle.
      Only one way forward: let the words guide themselves.
See where they take you and hope to find meaning among them.
   What at first looks like chaos can often conceal peace.
          You simply have to look closer, beyond intent.
Want and need should not always produce the same outcome.
   To find meaning is to find yourself—if you find it well.
    See everything clearly by unwinding the chaos, and then
                          you'll know peace.

* * *

[June 2018]

As you can see, Warren was struggling to put his ideas on the page. He could move on to new stories but not from the unanswered questions he left behind. So, with his ideas exhausted, there was nothing left to do but write about the struggle to write.

I didn't understand the title's significance at first, but I figured it out eventually. Warren knew that he was obsessing over his ideas, which resulted in him manipulating what he wanted so it would feel like something he needed, like kneading dough until it's fit for a specific purpose. It was the only way for him to keep going until he found a satisfying conclusion. His mind wouldn't be at ease until he solved the chaos, and if he did, he would know what he truly needed. It was quite a vicious cycle of knowing what you're doing is hurting you but thinking it will provide relief sooner or later.

JULY 2018

With Warren's last upload only being a hundred words, including the title, I figured he was fatigued and would take a few months off from writing. That's how it seemed, anyway, judging from the contents of the poem. This was during a time when I was struggling with my own work, and I could feel the fatigue Warren had conveyed. Writing for *Pen&Pad* while also analysing Warren's stories started to affect me, and not in the positive way that I experienced early on. I was still churning out good content, but I was suffering from a lot of stress, and the symptoms were getting too much to bear.

For that reason, when Warren surprisingly uploaded a new story very early in July, I didn't immediately open it. Don't get me wrong, I really wanted to, especially given the title of this new story, which you'll see in a moment, but I knew I had to take a break. If not just for myself, but also for Warren because he'd have less pressure to upload. Perhaps then he'd be able separate the wants from the needs. So, for the time being, I turned away.

It had been over a year since meeting Warren, although it felt longer in my head. I hadn't gone a day without one of his stories lingering on my mind, so I wasn't confident I could stay away from Warren's folder. It was difficult to concentrate the first few days, but as I became more absorbed in my own work, nothing else crossed my mind. It was freeing in a sense, but it also left me starved for something I couldn't figure out.

The magazine I wrote for often featured a story or two, but

it was fundamentally a tips and tricks guide to writing. What I personally liked to bring to it was the exploration of nuanced narrative and prose. One of the biggest differences I noticed in my writing was how easy it had been to produce content over the last year. As I said at the start, this book isn't about me, so I won't go into the specifics of my writing, but I feel it's important to mention because when I took a break from Warren's stories, my ideas started to dry up.

I couldn't see it at first, but after just one week, I started to notice how long it was taking me to think of new and interesting subject matters. And even when I managed to write something substantial enough to submit, it was lacklustre compared to the work I had done that cited Warren while exploring certain topics. Even the editor was starting to question the drop in quality.

It wasn't just my writing that had improved since meeting Warren: I also saw positive changes within myself. I was interested in my job for the first time in a long time and even started buying copies of the magazine again. I realised just how much Warren inspired me through both his positives and negatives, but it was clear there was a price to pay for that inspiration. Much like Warren, I would have to endure mental fatigue to bring out the best in myself. It was the only way that I could have a positive and meaningful influence on my readers. I needed to give them what Warren gave me while also giving back to Warren.

On the very last day of July, after almost three weeks, I gave in. These few paragraphs don't put it into perspective, but those weeks felt like months. My excitement grew quickly as I stepped back into *rename later* and picked up right where I'd left off.

A Day in the Life of a Serial Killer

I've been awake for what seems like a fortnight. I'm not sure how long a fortnight is at this point—two weeks, is it? Oh, what does it matter? The point is that I've lost track of time, and it's all his fault. My neighbour, that is. It all started... I don't know when it started, but it did at some point.

It must have been a Sunday because I was mowing the lawn. It's not much of a lawn and probably the smallest patch of grass for miles, save for the bits of moss growing up from under the paving slabs on the street. Why the council haven't sought to fix that yet is beyond belief. You know, one time I complained about a game of hopscotch that was drawn on the road because it looked unsightly, and you know what they did? They sent out two workers, not a brain cell between them, who drew a big yellow circle around it and then buggered off. It's been like that ever since.

Anyway, it was a Sunday. Well, I think it was. Either way, I was dumping grass into the bin when I noticed my neighbour stepping out of his house across the street. He placed several empty milk bottles into a cradle by the doorstep and looked around while taking in a deep breath. It was like he thought himself to be the star of his own TV series, and I was merely the background character.

For starters, I would never be a background character. I'd be a supporting character at absolute worst but never a background one. And who uses a milkman these days? Who is he trying to impress? If you want to impress me, don't stop there. Buy your own cow, name it, make friends with it, and train it to milk itself while you nap in your hammock. If that alone won't make people gush, then you could tell them how you're saving the planet by having your own personal cow squeeze its tit over your cornflakes to save on bottle production. You'll be the talk of the town. People will come from all over to witness your bovine benevolence. They'll cheer as you teach Susie the cow to read and bake so you can have cookies, milk and a bedtime story to sate your ego. But that's all for show. Your real scheme would be to defy your dad, who used to gleefully butcher all kinds of defenceless animals right before your eyes. Beef was his absolute favourite. Look at him now, Dad. Just look. As livid as this made me, it was merely a minor irritation compared to what happened next.

I was wheeling in my mower when I heard a nasal voice call out. I can't remember what was said, but I turned around in response and found my arrogant neighbour at the end of my driveway with a big smile spread across his cheeks. The audacity of this man to approach me after his display of arrogance. He was also wrapped in a fuzzy bathrobe and had his feet stuffed into slippers that looked as though they wanted to scream out in pain. And had they done, I just might have tried to save them from that pain. Only I could empathise with that kind of pressure as my neighbour edged closer towards me.

I had the mower at the ready. I had no idea what my plan was, but I was prepared to wrap thirty-six kilograms of a steel four-stroke engine around this man's skull if he tried anything funny. A machine like that is highly efficient in economic conservation and anatomic persuasion. Realistically, I'd struggle to lift that kind of weight even an inch off the ground, but don't underestimate how disabling it would be to have that mower rolled over your toes. I've done it to myself on one occasion, obviously by accident, and I was confined to my bed for almost an hour.

My neighbour stood there smiling, so I asked what he wanted. His name is Frank, by the way. I should've mentioned that. Referring to him as "neighbour" all the time gets tiresome. Well, I think his name was Frank. Yes, I'm sure. Maybe Hank. We'll go with Hank because it saves me typing one more letter each time I refer to him.

So, this grinning buffoon looked me dead in the eye, and he said, 'Lovely weather to cut some grass.'

I was beside myself with anger. Had I not been cutting grass, would he have popped over to state what awful weather it is to not cut the grass? Or, in his mind, does someone have to be mowing for there to be good weather outside? Are they not independent of one another?

I thought about it for just a second or two in the moment. His statement alone was subject to many questions, but his accusatory tone only begged further analysis. How dare he arouse suspicion on my property. Who on earth does this man think he is to be questioning my maintenance routine? As though it's so common to mow on such a day that any person with something to hide would use that as cover.

I didn't want to give Hank any other excuses to investigate me, so I chuckled in response. It was a bit delayed, but I think I played it off well because he left shortly after I broke into a huge belly laugh. And that was that; however, something stuck with me from that day. I couldn't quite figure out what it was at the time, but it irritated me to my core.

I kept an eye on him the next day when he got home from work. I think he's a dentist. I'm not sure why, and I have no evidence to back this theory—he just has one of those smiles. It's like he's advertising something. Good dental hygiene, perhaps. It was this thought that helped me realise what was really bothering me. This lonely man across the street, who never once had a visitor and conversed only with his milkman and stray cats, was always happy. And I mean always.

This man, who apparently calls himself Hank despite it

not being his real name, has never been seen without at least a smile. I say at least because sometimes he laughs to himself like a madman. I've never seen him convey a hint of sadness or anger. Once I thought I saw him frowning a little, but then he sneezed and burst with a satisfied smile. None of that is normal.

I started to doubt myself a little. Surely I had seen him without a smile just once, right? Was I just picking out memories that suited my own narrative? No, surely not. The only way I could settle this was by monitoring him very closely—from a distance, of course. If his happiness was truly unwavering, something more sinister was at play. I just hoped I was wrong.

Considering Hank claimed to be a dentist, I assumed he'd be up early in the morning to prepare for the day. I did some research and discovered most dental practices in the area had appointment bookings from eight, so I figured Hank would get there for seven to prep for his patients, meaning he would need to leave a little after six to beat the traffic. Logically he would need an hour to shower, get dressed and eat breakfast, so that meant he would be up at five. I woke up at four just to look out for any other potential activity.

Five o'clock came and went. Not much happened, but I noticed his recycling bin was still on the street. Collection for waste was on Thursday, and recycling and food were on Friday. If I had indeed mowed the lawn on Sunday, it was now Monday morning, so that bin had no right to be on the street. I considered the possibility of it being a simple mistake, but then I noticed that the food bin was nowhere in sight, which could only mean the recycling bin was left there deliberately.

What was Hank trying to achieve with this arrogant display? It was like a big middle finger to the whole neighbourhood. We get it, Hank. You recycle. You are the pinnacle of goodness in a sea of putrid opportunism. I bet you don't even change your bathwater right away. You probably wait until it matches the colours on the bottom row of the Dulux reference chart you pinned on the wall. Walnut cream puts you on the fence, but if it's Vandyke brown, that plug is pulled out like a weed. When it's been a particularly busy week poking and prodding gum and bone, out comes the forest palette because you suspect fungus green. That's probably why he doesn't have any visitors. He doesn't want them to see all the tea bags he puts on the radiators.

It was around half six when I finally saw some activity. The light went on in what I believe to be the living room, and if I've estimated the floor plan correctly, the layout is almost the exact reverse of my house. His kitchen faces the back garden, while mine faces the street. I hate it. I put up Roman blinds because I can't bare having the evening joggers poke their noses in at me while I'm at the sink. There I'll be in marigolds and a baking apron, scrubbing the life out of a saucepan, when a face drenched in sweat appears in the window with its mouth agape like cod on a hook. It's quite the sight.

I waited and watched. I was confident nothing would slip my gaze. I spied shadows move through every room as lights flicked on and off, but I couldn't get a clear look at what was going on inside. I knew I had to get closer. I'd never be able to see his misdeeds from such a distance, so I quietly went out into the front garden and crouched behind the hedge.

There was a noise across the road—like a shriek, but muffled. I thought it might have been a fox because they were often a nuisance in the area, but then I considered it logically. There I was, skulking in my own garden to find evidence of my neighbour's guilt, and I happened to hear a scream. Without a doubt in my mind, I thought it might have possibly come from Hank's house, but he didn't own a pet fox. Not to my knowledge, anyway.

'How peculiar,' I whispered to myself.

It would only make sense if that blood-curdling scream

belonged to something more human than a fox. But there was no way he'd have found a chimpanzee because they weren't native in the UK, so maybe it was something less human than a primate but only slightly more human than a fox. There was only one creature on earth that could fit such a description.

'A cow!'

I peeked over the hedge to make sure nobody had heard me. It was all clear, save for the black cat peering over at me from under a parked car on the road. It looked rough like it had been in a fight, but that was irrelevant.

A cow was the perfect fit, given Hank's aforementioned plan to train one to impress people, and it would've been dead easy for him to take one from the nearby fields. Training it, however, would prove challenging. Any cow would be vocal about such a thing at first, hence all the screaming.

This theory almost made sense. Almost. The only hole in this plot was that cows can't scream. They can bellow, maybe even shriek, but they can't scream. The only conclusion was that the scream belonged to something more human than a canine, less human than a primate, but more human than cattle. The more I tried to narrow the evidence, the more confused I became. I started to think I hadn't figured out anything correctly, but thinking that I had nothing figured out was what helped me figure it out. I realised I had it backwards. This was not a human-like animal at all. It was an animalistic human.

Nothing else made sense.

The pieces were starting to fit together neatly. With my non-factual deductions, I had all the evidence I needed. Here's the story. The true story of Hank, the serial killer.

A Day in the Life of Hank, The Devious Dentist

Hank, a proud and skilled dentist, grew tired of his mundane job. Sure, it paid well enough to afford a milkman, but it was nowhere near enough to buy and train a cow. In his frustrations, he became desperate to find something that excited him—something that would get his heart palpitating and reinvigorate his spirit.

Under cover of darkness, Hank targeted late-evening joggers. He chose this species because they were more human than cows but less human than normal humans. Besides, the neighbours didn't take too kindly to joggers, so Hank was confident nobody would be looking his way when he snatched them from outside his house. It was risky enough to be exciting because they were locals, but it was safe enough to get away with as he didn't know them personally.

Having access to all sorts of sedatives, Hank quickly put his victims to sleep and bound and gagged them in the garage. He always allowed a few hours to pass to ensure the neighbours were all deeply asleep before he did his work. Some victims would find a way to remove their gag, but that would only allow them a couple of seconds to scream before Hank put them back to sleep. And it didn't matter how much they screamed because nobody was awake to hear it.

Using only manual tools, Hank would cut up his victims while they were sedated. It was truly sadistic, but he could only feel alive by doing things he completely despised. He also took pleasure in convincing everyone he was a kind-hearted local dentist when he was secretly a cold-hearted serial killer.

Hank was surgical in the dismemberment of a human body. You'd think it was solely down to his clinical skills, but he also took inspiration from his father, who had worked his whole life as a butcher. Growing up, Hank would watch his father very closely, and now he was melding his skills and observations and putting them to use.

His victims would be discarded one small piece at a time using food waste bags. He'd make sure not to overfill the caddy so that it was never inspected too much during the weekly bin collection. However, using the food caddy made him paranoid because he feared one of the local foxes would come sniffing around and ruin everything. He would never leave the caddy on the street a second more than required, unintentionally neglecting the recycling bin as a result.

Then, while taking out empty milk bottles one morning, Hank caught his neighbour across the street watching him. Was this an isolated occurrence, he wondered, or had his neighbour always been watching? Hank tried to act as naturally as he could, but his neighbour still gave him the side-eye. He went over to greet him and instil some trust, but his robotic demeanour only aroused suspicion. He could see it in his neighbour's eyes. Hank knew he was exposed.

That day he devised a plan to lure out his neighbour under cover of night and turn him into his latest victim.

So there I was, having solved everything without a single loose end, sweating profusely and trembling behind my well-maintained hedge. I refused to be led like a cow to slaughter. Hank must have been watching me from his window. Or maybe he was in his garden, prone behind the knee-high wall. I didn't have much time. I spun around and ran back inside, spinning a second time before closing the door to confuse him.

It was close, but I managed to get back to safety.

I was now at a disadvantage. With Hank knowing that I know, without me having any tangible evidence to take to the authorities, I was a sitting duck. My only option was to catch him out. I couldn't leave until I had some video evidence of his crimes. I knew he'd be waiting for me if I left my house, so my only option was to barricade myself inside until his attention gets drawn to a new victim, where I would be ready.

I've been here for weeks now. A fortnight, maybe. I'm not sure. I've yet to catch Hank in the act, but I know I'm getting close because he's resumed his normal routine, going to and from work on a consistent schedule. It's only a matter of time before he forgets I'm watching and goes back to his hobby—his dirty little secret. I'll see behind that smile of his. I'll wipe it straight from his face.

I knew he didn't have a reason to smile so much.

Nobody does.

I'll prove it.

I'll show him.

There's no way out of this.

※ ※ ※

[July 2018]

Before this story, we were left with the notion that unwinding the chaos would provide some peace. This latest upload, however, wants to embrace as much chaos as possible and negate all sense of peace.

It was clear that Warren had decided to take our conversations and conceptualise them within a story of an obsessive neighbour. I see this protagonist as an exaggeration of Warren himself—not from his own perspective but from what he believes to be my interpretation of him. He thinks I see him as a recluse who is illogical in their conclusions and constantly suspicious of people who get too close. But that couldn't have been further from the truth, and it genuinely upset me that he believed I saw him this way.

After all the feedback I'd given him up to this point, I completely understood why he thought this way. But, on the other side, he completely misconstrued the bigger picture I saw. This was his way of convincing himself that I had inflated opinions so he could avoid facing his issues. That said, I do take some responsibility here. I still think everything I told him was right, but I understand now that it was too much at once. I should've given him room to grow on his own before offering my advice.

I decided to be more reserved in my emails from this point onwards. I still wanted to guide him in the right direction, but pushing him too hard only prompted him to push back.

The story itself was actually quite funny throughout, but it's clear how little passion was put into it. It felt rushed and lacked the complexity I was used to experiencing in Warren's other stories. I had impacted his work in such a negative way, and I knew I had to fix it.

I sent Warren an apology instead of my typical breakdown and feedback. I told him I understood the message conveyed through his latest upload and that we needed a fresh start. He didn't believe I fully understood at first, but he accepted my apology once I explained it in more depth.

OCTOBER 2018

Three months had passed since I last heard from Warren. I convinced myself he was just busy writing story after story, creating a compilation ready to show off, but that was way too optimistic, even for me. I hoped my apology would renew something in him, but I realised he'd need more time and patience to rediscover his passion for writing, which was evident when his next upload came along, as it was a week's worth of writing. Either he took the approach of quality over quantity way too seriously, or nothing had changed in the way he was thinking.

The Reaper's Commission

A Matter of Time

Here you are, old and tired;
Weary eyes and dreams uninspired.
As day turns to night, you just can't sleep;
Doubt begins to grow with thoughts buried deep.

Not even the sky shows speckles of light,
And so you wonder what's happened to your sight.
How could you miss signs so plain?
Can't you recall listening to the rain?

Now you see your senses are little,
And what about that body that had grown so brittle?
You still believe that the sun will soon rise.
Enough is enough; this isn't the place for hopeless lies.

This isn't a dream, and your mind doesn't plot.
In fact, it's right where you left it and has started to rot.
It's not shadow you witness nor starless sky;
This here is the peace you have yearned for, so don't be shy.

The sun can't rise because it is you who has set;
Don't worry about the past, as you'll soon forget.
Absence of light is nothing to fear;
Emotion is for those above, not us down here.

THE REAPER'S COMMISSION

The sun will rise again, but not for you.
All will fade alongside the life that you knew.

Come now; eternity won't wait,
And I warn that Death despises those who are late.
For he is also old and tired;
Aching bones and hope expired.

Reach out for the cloak of black,
And you'll finally see there's no going back.
From here, you'll sink, though you'll desperately try to climb.
But you can't escape Death once he has you, for his weapon is time.

The hooded figure was pacing up and down the dusty room with a sheet of paper clasped in its fleshless hands. There was no sign of light underneath its hood, just a black cavity that grew when eyes looked upon it, and that's precisely why Adam was looking down at the rotten bones of the figure's feet.

'I don't know,' said the figure. 'It makes me sound weak.'

Adam shifts his gaze up to the black robes. 'Well, I was trying to convey a sense of morbid discomfort.'

'Yeah, I get that. But "old and tired"? It makes me sound like a has-been. You know I don't age, right? I'm the Grim Reaper, not Grandad Grim.'

'It's not meant to be literal. It conveys that you're bound to the rules of time, much like us.'

'But I'm not, and my bones don't ache. They creak a little, but I don't feel aches or pains like you lot.'

'Again,' Adam said, putting his hands together, 'it's not literal.'

'Don't do that here,' the figure ordered.

Adam threw his hands down without a blink.

'I like the rhymes,' the figure calmly continued.

Adam's gaze dropped to his own feet. 'That's great, Mister Reaper. I'm glad.'

'I'm not your substitute teacher. Call me Grimmer—I'm trying to get it to stick.'

Adam didn't respond.

'You're not mad, are you?'

'I'm not mad,' Adam softly replied.

'It might've been better without the italic font. It's a bit annoying to read like that.'

'Noted.'

'They're not all like that, are they?'

'Mostly, yeah.'

'At least you know for next time.'

'Sure.'

Grimmer hands the paper to Adam. 'What else have you got for me?'

A Day in the Life of Death

No clocking in, no clocking out,
No benefits or salary to brag about.
A service owed, endless debt to pay.
An eternity of work, no time to play.

—

'I get some downtime now and then,' Grimmer said, looking up from the paper, 'and what would I do with a salary anyway? I've got plenty of robes, and I don't collect objects because I'm not possessive—not in that way, at least. I like what your kind would call... minimalism.'

Adam sighed. 'Finish reading it first.'

Grimmer looked back down at the paper.

—

Not a moment to ponder, not a minute to feel.
Collections and deliveries, endless cards to deal.

—

Grimmer paused again and said, 'I don't actually deal the cards. That's a job for fate, and I wouldn't want to piss it off. You'll understand if you ever meet it.'

Adam's jaw was starting to ache. 'It's not meant to... I can explain after. Just keep reading until you get to the end.'

'I can't. It's already off to a bad start, and I just can't see myself in this, you know?'

Adam resists snatching the sheet of paper and receives it with a tightened grip. Grimmer stretches its arms—it would've yawned if it had lungs—and then picks up another sheet from a dwindling stack of paper on the table.

The reaper reaps but does not sow,
And he plays for keeps but keeps on the low.
Counting all the sheep 'cause a sheep heap will always follow,
but their sleep ain't deep 'cause the pills were weak, and they were hard to swallow.
Thoughts start to creep, but secretly it's a truth they already know.
Now they see that the pain won't ease 'cause, partially, their souls are on show.

—

'Is this a rap?' Grimmer asked.

'I was going for something modern,' Adam replied,

scratching the back of his head.

'You're just not good at it, to be honest.'

'I'm new to multi-syllabic rhymes. I thought I'd give it a go.'

'This is the kind of stuff you show your mum before anyone else.'

Adam didn't respond. His head sunk lower than ever as he picked up the next sheet of paper.

Small Heart

My God...

What big eyes you have.

All the better to see my children.

And what big ears you have.

All the better to hear their prayers.

And... my God, what a small heart you have.

All the better to ignore them.

Adam held his breath as Grimmer pondered over the sheet in its hand.

'Half of this isn't bad,' Grimmer finally said.

Adam perked up. 'Which half?'

'The bits that aren't in italics.'

'So just the bits that insult God,' Adam replied, his posture deflating.

'Ah yeah, that's why I like it.' Grimmer tilted its head and brought the sheet closer to its cavity. 'Big eyes, big ears—sounds like a tarsier. Have you ever seen one of them? You should look it up later.'

Adam stares.

'I've seen one,' Grimmer continued, 'but only once, though. A dead one, actually. Big mix-up, don't even ask.'

Adam held up a new sheet.

Have you ever?

Have you ever seen a face so plain?
A weakened spirit soaked with rain.

Have you ever noticed a mask so thin?
Sadness beneath a withering grin.

Have you ever witnessed so much imperfection?
That person you don't recognise staring back in your reflection.

'I don't get this one at all,' Grimmer said. 'I don't have a reflection.'

'Reflection? Where does it say that?' Adam looked at the paper, and his eyes widened. 'That's not supposed to be in there.'

Grimmer looked at Adam, then at the poem, and then at Adam again. 'Why not?'

Adam took the sheet and shoved it into his pocket. 'No reason.'

'Oh, I see. Are you... okay? Is there anything you want to talk about?'

'No, that's just practice, that's all.'

'You can tell me—I'll listen. You'd have to be quick, though, because I have to get back to work soon.'

'There's nothing to talk about,' Adam said, checking what was written on the next sheet of paper. 'There's still plenty to read, though.'

Here, lies.

Down in the trench, idly sat,
Was a tired young soldier unstrapping his hat.
He looked through his rations and found some bread,
Then he turned and offered a piece to his friend lying dead.
An offer met with an expression so dull,
So the piece went to the friends that crawled inside his friend's skull.

Panic around him, yet no one did speak;
Not even the rats had let out a squeak.
A noise in the air, as though a whistle was blown;
If his eardrums had ruptured, he wouldn't have known.
The sky began to spin, and he became unstable,
Like a bowl losing its shape on a potter's turntable.

There came a dim light, then a large silhouette;
A hand was extended, and a voice said, 'Up you get.'
The soldier took the hand and was pulled to his feet,
Then he put his palm on his chest, feeling for a beat.
The silhouette laughed and pointed straight ahead;
When the soldier lifted his chin, he realised he was dead.

"Here lies the forgotten" had been carved into rock;
The soldier turned pale and started to shake with the shock.
Wind filled the air, and shadow danced with the light;
The soldier dropped to his knees and lost all strength to fight.
Darkness became heavy and started growing all around;
Not one word could be spoken as the soldier was dragged under the ground.

'Morbid,' Grimmer said.

'So you like it?' Adam asked with a hesitant smile.

'It's the best of the lot, I guess. Wasn't expecting the end. That's not how people go to hell, but creative license and all that.'

Adam rolled his eyes.

'I'll assume the soldier was on the bad side,' Grimmer continued. 'Whatever side that is, or was. Time doesn't exist here, so I guess it doesn't matter. Anyway, this will have to do for now. I need to get back to work.'

'So... I get to go back? Like we agreed?'

'Not now. I lost track of time. Just keep working on a few more until I get back to see if you can top this one, and then we'll talk about it.'

Grimmer faded into the shadows. Adam had wanted to speak up but feared he'd be left alone forever if he did. He pulled out a blank sheet of paper from the bottom of the stack and paused for a moment. He stared into the white page, simply enjoying the view of a clean slate before he put darkness into something so pure.

* * *

[October 2018]

It turned out that, in a way, Warren had indeed been working on a compilation of work, only it was within one story. This was similar to *The Perfect Twist* but far darker in tone and theme. Comparing the two stories demonstrates how Warren had changed over time and how his views on the industry were warped by his fear of failure—of not being good enough. Both narratives share a commentary on criticism, but *The Reaper's Commission* fails to overcome the pressure and submits to it instead.

In the story, Grimmer nitpicks faults in Adam's work, clearly missing the point of each one and taking them far too literally. It was frustrating for Adam, but he kept quiet because he needed the approval of Grimmer before he could move on. This could've been a simple dig at audience expectations, but I think it was more likely that Warren was externalising his own doubts about his work.

By the end, Adam was left staring at a sheet of paper, unwilling to dirty its surface. From that, I could only assume Warren was trying to show me that the more he wrote, the less he wanted to write. It would explain why he was taking longer to finish a single story, but he clearly didn't understand why he felt this way. If only he had listened to me from the beginning. I could've helped him out of his head before it got to this stage.

Warren's stories were now focused on fear, paranoia, death, and decay. It's a dark mindset to live in when you're writing with such heavy themes. It wasn't Warren's style. It wasn't him at all.

NOVEMBER 2018

Throughout this month, I mulled over an idea that led to the development of this book. It only started with the plan of putting Warren's work together as a book of short stories to show him at his best. I wanted to get Warren's permission first, but I figured it would only distract him, so I planned to finish a final draft before telling him about it. It quickly proved to be a good decision because it only took until the end of November for him to upload a new story.

The Unexamined Life
Part IV: Your Worst Enemy

Jimmy stares out the window, watching the waves reach up to the sky and fall down with a crash. He can't sit still—it feels as though thorns and grit had been mixed into the upholstery of the armchair.

His eyes dart around the room, and he notices that the wallpaper is covered with cracks and dust, its colour now void of any vibrancy.

The phone barely makes more than and chirp before Jimmy snatches it up.

'So, what next?' The Counsellor says.

'I've no idea,' Jimmy replies. 'I'm beginning to feel hopeless.'

'Stop that. We've invested too much time now. There must be something you're suited to. Why can't you be like the rest of them?'

'In what way?'

There's no answer.

Jimmy puts his ear closer to the phone. 'Hello?'

'Never mind,' The Counsellor finally replies. 'So, you weren't happy with the lack of recognition as a practitioner, and you were unsettled by the confines of the law.'

'It's a bit more complicated than that.'

'What I think,' The Counsellor continues, 'is that you want to help and inspire at the same time, with your name known by many but not millions. Meaningful work on a smaller scale.'

'You sound like you have an idea already.'

'I do. I think you should try being a teacher. A university lecturer, to be specific.'

PART IV: YOUR WORST ENEMY

'But what would I even teach?'

'Definitely not medicine or law,' The Counsellor says. 'Arts and humanities?'

Jimmy nibbles his lip. 'Isn't that a bit... broad?'

'We're making the rules here. We will reinvent the role of a lecturer, and you can teach a broad range of subjects, from history to... probably not religious studies, but to linguistics, literature, and so on.'

'But I don't know anything about that stuff.'

'Who does?'

'Lecturers.'

The Counsellor clears his throat loudly and says, 'Everything you'll need will be in the textbooks. Everything there is to teach is already set in stone—it's not like it's made up on the spot. Lecturers teach what they've been taught by those who have learnt from those who taught them. They know as much as the next guy, and there's no room for opinions in class. You know all this, so just keep regurgitating information and students will love and remember you for it. They will cite you as the main reason for their successes.'

'I get that this can be an inspiring role, but—'

'Great!' The Counsellor bursts out. 'Off you go then, it's all ready.'

There's a click, and the dial tone starts. Jimmy keeps the handset against his ear and listens to the hum with his eyes set on the agitated waves. It all begins to merge into a state of entrancement, and he feels the weight of the sea against his skin, with the hushing—

The dial tone cuts out. 'Forgo the introspection, Jimmy,' The Counsellor says. 'It's boring. Just go.'

The students turn their attention to Jimmy as soon as he steps into the classroom. Jimmy pictures them as one collective gawking eye, suspended in a void between daydreams and anxiety.

'Good morning, everyone,' Jimmy says.

'Good afternoon,' a few of the students reply together.

'Afternoon, eh,' Jimmy mutters as he stops at his desk, eyeing a textbook titled "A Guide to Textbooks".

Another script. The thought of going through it is exhausting enough. It doesn't have to be that way, though, Jimmy ponders. He knows he's in full control.

He holds up the book for the class to see. 'Does everyone have one of these with them?'

There are some affirmative mumbles and positive nods, but none of them directly speak up.

'Great,' Jimmy continues, 'now put it away—in your bag or just down by your feet.'

The students hesitantly follow the instruction.

'Today, you get the freedom of choice. Together you'll decide on what you'll be learning, and it can be anything you want. Anything but textbooks. Sound good?'

One student puts his hand up, raising it no higher than his frizzy hair.

Jimmy points at him. 'Yes?'

'That's not exactly giving us the freedom of choice,' the student replies.

'What's your name?'

'Joe.'

'How so, Joe?'

'You've just limited our choices. So yeah, we have freedom of the choice, but we're restricted in what we can choose.'

'I haven't limited anything. I told you to choose whatever you want.'

'You said anything except textbooks,' Joe argues.

'Well... yeah, why would you want to learn about textbooks? That doesn't even make sense.'

'I didn't say I did. I'm just questioning your idea of freedom of choice.'

Jimmy looks at the other students.

They're all listening intently, waiting for his rebuttal with

PART IV: YOUR WORST ENEMY

their pens in hand.

'The textbook itself represents the idea of restrictions,' Jimmy offers.

'But removing it from the debate is a restrictive idea,' Joe counters.

Jimmy sits on the edge of his desk and folds his arms, exactly how he's seen in a few television shows.

'Anyone else feel this way?' Jimmy asks, looking left and right, up and down.

'I do,' a girl at the top of the room replies.

'What's your name?'

'Kim.'

'Kim, with the bedhead, you don't think the textbooks are restrictive?'

'That's not the question,' Kim quickly answers. 'It's like saying, you can pick any colour to draw with that isn't blue. It's an illusion of free choice. And my hair is just naturally wavy.'

'You don't really need another example,' Jimmy replies. 'The actual situation is enough. In fact, this situation is a better example to get your point across than the example you gave. You just simplified it, which undermines not just your own intelligence but everyone else's in the room too. You've also wasted time when you could've gone into more detail about your actual opinion rather than... you know what, it doesn't matter. Anyone else either agree or even disagree? Start with your name because, to be honest, I'm getting really lazy. Maybe even just say something visually unique about yourself, like your hair. People enjoy that—makes their imagination work less. More so-called restrictive freedom of choice for you.'

'I'm Scott and—'

'Speak up.'

'I'm Scott,' the timid boy to the left of the room repeats, no louder than before, 'and I've got... black hair?'

Jimmy shakes his head.

'Short black hair?'

'Short greasy black hair with a cow lick at the front will do, thanks.'

Scott slouches a bit lower. 'Anyway, I guess there's a spectrum where levels of freedom exist, and society is an example of that. If we had true freedom to choose whatever, we'd have anarchy.'

'A bit extreme. That doesn't really apply, buddy. I'm not asking for a philosophical analysis of society. Any less dramatic opinions from anyone?'

'Hey, I'm Zara. I have long black hair, and I guess it's... shiny?'

Jimmy cranes his neck forward and squints. 'We'll go with waxy. A little bit flat, too. Void of life, even.'

'Sure. Anyway, I think you're using your personal negative view of textbooks to rule it out as a choice, which just isn't fair. There might be people here who prefer guidance from a textbook, and you disguising a limitation as free choice is a bit... dishonest.'

'You think I'm lying to you?'

'I think you're lying to yourself.'

Jimmy's eyes widen with a realisation, one that quickly falls to his stomach and causes an ache.

'What's wrong?' Zara asks. 'I didn't mean to offend you or anything.'

Jimmy scans the room and spots a student looking down at his mobile. He leaps up the steps and snatches it from his hands.

'I need to make one call,' Jimmy says, running for the door.

He starts dialling and kicks his way into the corridor.

'What's wrong, Jimmy?' The Counsellor answers.

'It's not working out.'

'What? It was going fine. What could possibly be wrong now?'

PART IV: YOUR WORST ENEMY

'Let me through, and I'll explain.'

The Counsellor sighs. 'Go through the fire exit ahead of you.'

Jimmy doesn't even bother to sit on the chair and snatches the phone from its cradle.

'You know you should be sitting,' The Counsellor says.

'Why can't I leave?' Jimmy asks.

'What do you mean, leave?'

'Leave! Leave here!'

'I've explained before—a while back.'

'You said I can't leave, but I get the freedom to choose anything I want to be.'

'Right.'

'That's not freedom.'

'Not freedom?' The Counsellor says in a hardened tone. 'You can literally be whatever you want to be.'

'Except free, right? You've already decided the outcome for me. No matter what I choose, I'm still here. That's what you want, not me.'

'Yes, you are here, and you do get a choice. I just stopped you from making a mistake, and that's the whole point of why I'm here.'

Jimmy tightens his grip on the handset. 'Why are you so sure you know what's best for me?'

'Why are you so sure you know what's best for yourself?'

'I don't, but I'd rather be in control and fail than be any kind of puppet.'

'So that's what you really want, Jimmy? To be in control? Well, you've always been in control. You just haven't realised it because you've spent too much time staring at windows.'

Jimmy looks out at the cluster of dark clouds forming above a thrashing ocean. The miserable and trying weather provokes something in Jimmy, and he finally understands The Counsellor's words. The ache in his stomach fades.

'Is that double glazing?' he asks.

The Counsellor doesn't reply.

Jimmy stares at the handset while taking a couple of steps back. He squeezes it into his palm, takes a deep breath, and launches it at the window like a baseball. It hits the glass with a thud, and the pane erupts with a wave of cracks that spread out in every direction. He walks up to the window and lightly brushes his fingertips over one of the larger fractures. He presses a little harder, and splinters of glass fall to the floor, leaving behind small gaps that break up the image of the ocean like an incomplete puzzle.

Jimmy returns to the table with a smile and picks up the phone cradle. He slowly takes another deep breath, holds it, and then hurls the cradle at the window with a passionate roar. Two layers of glass burst into pieces, and the sky and ocean crumble away before his very eyes, revealing a single corridor that stretches into the distance.

The white floors and walls are ignited in bright light, almost like a set for a sitcom based inside a hospital. Jimmy steps onto the unembellished tiles and realises the corridor branches into many other endless corridors, all of which have turnings of their own. Jimmy stares in awe. It's overwhelming, but it's also freedom. Freedom to choose any direction and venture into the unknown at the risk of never finding the way back. Where there are consequences for every choice made. And in his head, Jimmy concludes that's exactly what he needs.

Even with a choice of endless directions, instinct drives him in only one, and that's forward. Safe but promising. And so he walks. He passes countless branches of corridors that all tempt him to turn in their direction, but he doesn't take any of them because he wants whatever's at the end of the path he's on now. It's the safest bet, or so he keeps telling himself. He's convinced it will pay off, despite the doubts in the back of his mind urging him to turn back.

PART IV: YOUR WORST ENEMY

It's only in our most desperate moments that we're truly tested. Because in those moments, regrets pour in, and you think that maybe it's better to give up sooner than later. Why bother dragging it out if you're destined to fail no matter how hard you try? Why not save yourself some pain? It's easier that way. Easier to give up.

A blurred image appears directly ahead of Jimmy, so he rubbishes the thought of giving up and bursts into a run. The image begins to take the shape of a door. He stumbles to a stop and stares at it, analysing its surface. There's something peculiar about it. He grabs the brass handle and pauses at its cold touch. It's uncomfortably familiar, like a stranger on the street calling you by name, insisting you've met before.

Jimmy timidly opens the door and steps inside, stopping in shock. An armchair, a table, a telephone, bright green wallpaper—had he gone in a circle? He was sure it was a straight walk. And then he notices the large window with a view of a lonely swing at the bottom of a garden. A garden he knows. The kind of garden many people would know, and it was all separated by a single layer of glass. Jimmy hesitantly walks over to the armchair, but his apprehension fades when he sits down and stares outside.

He anticipates a phone call, preparing his nerves for the startling rattle, but it doesn't come. He rests his fingertips on the handset, tempting it to ring, but nothing happens. He snatches up the handset in annoyance and puts it to his ear. A ringtone starts and quickly ends.

'Hello?' a familiar voice softly answers.

Jimmy's heartbeat becomes rapid, and he wonders if all those doubts were warnings in disguise.

'You wanted to talk, Jimmy,' Jimmy replies in a voice just as soft.

* * *

[November 2018]

I reread the first three parts of this story before this new entry just so I didn't miss any connections. For a story that appears sporadic in its production, its resolution comfortably brings it full circle.

Part IV reveals how Warren was feeling at the time. I think The Viewing Room started to change to reflect how his mind had developed between parts, showing he was more aware of his struggles than I realised. Jimmy becomes more uncomfortable due to these changes, alongside the growing impatience of The Counsellor. Even before the implications of the ending, there's a sense these two characters are one in the same—two perceptions of one mind. If Jimmy is the aspiration, The Counsellor is the self-motivation.

Once Jimmy is inside the classroom, Warren's disregard for technique is more prevalent than ever. He refuses to use description during narration and instead uses Jimmy to push characters into describing themselves. This could've been genuine laziness, but writing it this way is more time-consuming. It isn't exactly out of place, though, as every part of this story has this element, but it had become tiresome because I hoped Warren would've embraced some storytelling techniques by this point.

As expected, Jimmy's personality changes once again, and this time he's very cruel towards the students he's supposed to be teaching. Like I said after the other parts, I think this is to reflect a personal experience of Warren's. He wouldn't write an unlikable protagonist without good reason. However, once Jimmy leaves the classroom, he's more like the person he was in *Part I*, setting up the climax of his journey.

The beginning of the end comes when Jimmy realises that his choices have always been limited, having been pushed in certain directions all his life. He rushes back to The Viewing

Room to take control, and then we get the reoccurring double glazing motif. I've tried to wrap my head around why there's so much emphasis on this, but only Warren can give any clarity on what it really means—if it means anything at all. If I were to guess, I'd say it's a hint that not everything is as it seems, hence why the final room is described with a single pane of glass right before the revelation.

Speaking of the revelation, I don't believe it's meant to have one meaning, but on its surface, it's about taking back control. If you expect things to go your way and achieve goals without merit, you'll be left standing still, watching as life passes you by. So, with a renewed sense of self, Jimmy takes back control of his life and discovers true freedom.

This story, all parts included, always brings me a sense of melancholy. I interpret its message as one of hope, but unlike Jimmy, Warren struggled to achieve the same freedom; he refused to stay on the safe path and got lost in the corridors instead.

JANUARY 2019

I started the first draft of this book during the first week of January, and the more I worked on it, the more my ideas expanded. Eventually, I no longer wanted to produce a simple compilation of work; I wanted to include my thoughts to add context to these stories, which developed into a story itself. I couldn't leave out Warren in all this, so I outlined as much information on him as possible and used it as a base to start from.

It was an exciting project at the time, mainly because this was before Warren stopped writing. All I could think about was how much he would appreciate my efforts. The only problem was that the story I needed to tell was ongoing. I had the beginning and the middle, but I had no idea what was next because it hadn't happened yet. Warren would ultimately shape its conclusion, which was, and still is, my biggest concern. Ideally, I want a positive ending with a message that will motivate Warren and others like him, but I have no control over it. It's difficult to focus when no certainties lie ahead, but I continue to write this book with the hope I get my conclusion.

Once again, Warren uploaded another story by the end of the month. Or, in a way, he didn't upload a story at all. That'll make sense in just a moment.

A Tale Untold

The Forlorn Valley hadn't seen growth for years, save for a scattering of weeds. The land was dry, desolate, and rather sad to look at. If you were standing on top of the northern ridge looking south to its lowest point, you wouldn't notice a thing. Not in the literal sense, but in the sense that nothing significant would catch your eye. None of that matters, though, because you'd never find yourself there to not notice anything. However, if you were on top of that northern ridge looking to the south, for whatever reason, it would shock you to know there was a lot going on in the distance.

You would never be able to tell from so far away, and the only way you would find out is if you were to explore every part of this valley and its weeds until you come across a tired old man digging up dirt with his hands. Unfortunately, it would be highly improbable for you to have explored this valley on the exact day and hour that would have you collide with this stranger.

It's a tale that could never be told, so there's little point in me telling it. But I'm going to anyway. So if the unlikely were to happen, and you did come across a tired old man digging with his hands in the middle of a dead valley, you'd want to ask him a question or two. Perhaps you'd not even greet him and simply ask what on earth he's doing. He'd stand up and turn around to face you. You'd see that his face is bright red, scorched by the sun. You'd see that his clothes are worn and covered with dust. And most importantly, you'd see the blank stare in his eyes and perceive it as emptiness.

'Are you okay?' you might ask upon seeing his state.

Or maybe you show little concern for this man's well-being and say, 'Are you mad?'

You could even say nothing at all because the stranger's answer would be the same no matter what you do.

He'd look you dead in the eye and ask, 'Would you like to help me?'

Yes, he'd be serious. You wouldn't even have to ask, but you probably would anyway. Not that it would make a difference because the stranger wouldn't reply. He would pick up a sack you had failed to notice and hand it to you.

You might ask what's inside before opening it, or you could open it without hesitation. It wouldn't make a difference because what's inside the sack wouldn't change either way. No matter what, you'd open the bag and find a young potted tree. You could ask what type of tree, but you don't know anything about trees, so why would you care? Or maybe you do know a lot about trees, but in this moment, the striking image of an old man planting a healthy tree in a dry and barren valley would beg more questions. The stranger would suspect your curiosity and gesture to the hole he'd dug.

'You're planting it here?' you might ask him, despite the answer being plainly obvious. Or you'd simply stare, not fully comprehending the logic of the unlikely situation you've found yourself in.

The stranger would take the tree from you, free it from its pot, and then hand it back. You'd instinctively accept it, making sure to support the earth that held together the tree's roots. At this point, you'd probably feel it necessary to inform the stranger that the tree has no hope of surviving these conditions, but you'd also wonder how useful your advice would be to a man so seemingly lost. So you would instead reach down and place the young tree inside the hole, and the stranger would gently pat it down with some earth.

'Take care,' the stranger would say, turning his back to you.

You wouldn't be able to let him go without finding a reason for this odd event, so you'd think of an easy question that would only require a simple but effective answer.

So you'd ask, 'Why plant a tree here when it's likely to die?'

The man would turn back with an honest smile. 'Why are you here helping me to plant a tree that's likely to die?' the stranger would respond.

You might take a moment to think about his response. Or you might quickly counter it and say, 'That's not why I came here at all.'

And if you did, the stranger would ask, 'Why else would you be here?'

It would be impossible to answer because you wouldn't be there. There would be no reason for it—unless that reason was to help this stranger plant a tree. So maybe he had to be here planting a tree, and if he were not, this moment would have never occurred, even though it didn't. But if it had, the only reason to be in this moment would be to plant a tree that's likely to die, or you would not be here to question it.

The stranger would notice your struggle to comprehend the situation you're not really in, and he'd offer you clarity.

'See what's around you,' he would say.

You might question why, but it wouldn't make a difference because every possible question you could ask would lead to you following his instruction. But when you look around, you see the same desolate valley and scattering of weeds described at the beginning of this tale. You wouldn't need to speak because your face would convey your lack of realisation to the stranger.

'No,' he would say as soon as you looked back at him. 'Don't look with the mind. See with your eyes.'

You wouldn't have ever considered the difference before

now, and suddenly you'd let words like desolate and dry free from your internal monologue as you look upon the valley once again. And this time, you'd look for details that can be put into your own description. Instead of weeds, you'd notice small trees scattered around you, all similar to the tree you would've planted. Not just a few, but many that stretch into the distance. Instead of dry dirt, you'd see that the soil around those trees is healthy and vibrant. Instead of sadness, you'd feel joy. Instead of being in the middle of nowhere, you would now be here.

It wouldn't be a dream or trick of any kind. In fact, the stranger would reassure you that what you see is real and was there all this time. But that's not something you'd be able to accept right away, is it? You'd think you were hallucinating due to dehydration or some other logical explanation that would absolve your lack of perception. It wouldn't be conceivable in your mind that you were fooled by the introduction to this story.

You'd eventually come to accept the reality of the situation, but questions would still be lingering on your mind.

'Did you plant all these yourself?' is what you'd ask next, but probably not.

'No, these trees are part of other tales, not ours,' the stranger would reply.

In response, you might say, 'But why here?'

'Where else would you like these tales to take place?' the stranger would ask. 'They must take place somewhere. And if it was somewhere else, you'd ask the very same question.'

No matter how much the stranger explained, it wouldn't be enough.

With nothing else to say, you'd bid the stranger farewell.

You would leave that valley, but the valley would never leave you. You'd wonder what it would look like in ten years if somehow you found yourself on top of that northern ridge again. Would there be an endless sight of luscious trees? Each representing a moment in time—a tale each tree could never tell. And if that story could never be told, who's to say it ever happened?

You might tell yourself, 'I'm to say it happened. I was there.'

But you weren't there. You were never part of that stranger's story, let alone part of the many other moments that valley had seen. Because you didn't find yourself on top of that northern ridge, and you weren't there on that very same day at the very same hour that stranger planted his tree. You did not question his purpose or see the valley through your own eyes. You've only seen it through the description in this story.

For every tale there is, there is one that isn't.

This is one of those that will never be.

This tale was never told.

* * *

[January 2019]

This was a very strange read, and I know that's often been the case up until this point, one way or another, but this one felt different. I still struggle to understand what Warren was trying to convey in this story, but there's a hidden sense of dread underneath it all.

The two characters in this story don't really say or do much. They're used to pedal the message, which I think is a little lost somewhere in the narrative. My only understanding of it, at a surface level, is that the abandoned trees represent stories that have been written, but if those stories are never read, were they ever really told? It makes me think of this classic thought experiment: If a tree falls in the forest and no one is around to hear it, does it make a sound? I don't want to directly compare the two because this story is about a writer's motivation and not questions of observation or perception, but it helps to wrap your head around the metaphor.

It's a very cryptic story overall, and I'm sure there's a lot here I've missed, but it was enough to prove that Warren was at a crossroads. He was questioning if there was any point in writing if these stories weren't going to be read by anyone. And if nobody reads what he's written, did he truly write anything in the first place? It's a thought many of us go through—a thought of why do we pursue our passions if we cannot share them. And with what we've learned so far, we know Warren was anxious to put himself in front of an audience. He wanted people to experience his stories but feared the criticism that comes with it, which is a difficult trap to free yourself from. Not without help, anyway.

With all the evidence of Warren struggling mentally, I'm not sure why I hadn't anticipated him giving up. The last couple of stories before this one should've been a clear indication that he was going through something personal.

I just wanted him to be okay.

Maybe I could've done more to help him. Instead of constantly urging him to improve and progress, I could've encouraged him by telling him what he wanted to hear and giving him more praise. It's not the healthiest way forward, but sometimes it's all we need to get through a difficult time.

FEBRUARY 2019

This month marked two years since that writing festival—since meeting Warren for the first time. That same festival was running again this year, but I hadn't attended any events for several months. I wanted to go, but I was too busy poring over all these stories while sorting through my thoughts about it all. I didn't even know how to structure the book at this point, but I was making a lot of progress and was happy to put aside things that would've distracted me.

I figured Warren would take another couple of months to produce a new story, and that was fine because I already had plenty of material to pick apart. But then, just a week into February, a new story appeared. I don't know why I even checked the folder, but I couldn't stop myself—it was like an addiction. I knew that the more stories he sent, the more content I had for this book. I had already spent several months on it and was determined to finish it no matter how long it took.

One-ninety-five

Good morning, One-ninety-five. Your vitals look well. I can see that you need to void your bowels. You will have ten minutes to do so before you're expected downstairs for breakfast.

The confident yet soft voice in the air doesn't sound human, but it's close enough. A gaunt, hairless man in a blue jumpsuit sits up and throws his feet off the edge of a wall-mounted bed.

Nine minutes, One-ninety-five.

One-ninety-five stands up, throwing the bed sheet to the floor. The chains holding up the bed retract, folding the frame against the wall.

Eight minutes. Do not forget to brush your teeth.

One-ninety-five does as he's told within the time limit, and the electronic lock on the door clicks open.

Making his way down the hall, One-ninety-five peers into the other rooms. He does this every day despite knowing there's nobody else left. The rooms have stayed clean due to the automated maintenance, making them appear all the more lifeless. One-ninety-five often thought he would feel better if the rooms were unkempt and decrepit. He longs for something that reflects what's beyond the walls instead of being trapped inside a lie.

The canteen has a lingering odour of bleach so strong that One-ninety-five has to squint when entering. There are rows upon rows of benches shining brightly in the white light—not a spot of dirt to be found. Only one bench breaks up the symmetry because it features a cup of water and a plate of something you could only describe as undiscovered matter.

Your flavour today is potato, peas, and carrots. As usual, we remind you to drink all of your medicated water.

You have forty minutes for consumption. According to stool analysis, your digestion was not sufficient. We have identified stress as a major contributing factor and concluded you require more exercise—in body and mind. You will take one additional hour in the garden after breakfast, where you will be encouraged to move as much as possible, and then you will attend a stress management session this evening.

One-ninety-five takes a seat on the cold steel bench and stares down into the matter. It doesn't look pleasant. It never did. The smell, however, pleases the nose and sends a signal to the tongue that prompts a lick of the lips. It's quite a cruel trick. One-ninety-five knows it contains every bit of nutrition his body needs, but the sight of it disturbs the pit of his stomach.

It doesn't take him long to finish eating. It usually takes him fifteen minutes at most, but today it only takes ten. He uses the rest of his allotted time to stare at the wall with no thought or wonder in his head. He wouldn't know what to think about even if given a good suggestion. All that he could possibly give thought to had already been thought about, so there was nothing left for him to ponder. He simply stares at the wall and observes only the visual information: the subtle bumps and groves in the concrete, the glossy coat of white paint, and the sheer height it stood. He could tell you the textural properties of every surface in the canteen, though if you were to ask how it made him feel, you'd be met with a blank stare.

You may go out into the garden now, One-ninety-five.
You are encouraged to complete five laps of the perimeter

at a pace of your choosing.

It's only a short walk through a narrow corridor before One-ninety-five feels grass between his toes. The grass is artificial, but it's as good as real to him because it's all he's ever known. The feeling is pleasant enough in comparison to the hard and cold floors of the other rooms.

Apart from a warmer shade of light, the ceiling looks the same as the one in the canteen. It also sits at the same height and doesn't alleviate the anxiety of being helplessly trapped. The air conditioning, however, is considerably stronger here and provokes a sense of relief in One-ninety-five, although it's not enough to prompt a sigh.

You have two hours, One-ninety-five. As a reminder, you are encouraged to complete five laps of the perimeter at your own pace. Do not touch the walls, and do not cross any white lines marked on the grass.

One-ninety-five, at walking speed, begins his first lap. The perimeter provides adequate space but lacks any equipment or furniture. That's why all there is to do is walk, although it does help to speed up the time. Not that there's any rush. Whether he's in the garden, canteen, library, or cell, time is always spent waiting for time to pass.

...SOME TIME GOES BY...

There, see how quickly it goes. Two hours have gone just like that.

Your time is up, One-ninety-five. You can now spend the afternoon either in the library or the entertainment room.

One-ninety-five always chooses the library, although he never goes there to read. He used to, but now he only looks at the book covers and guesses what he might read should he ever feel the urge again. He doesn't even try reading the blurbs. You'd think he'd prefer to be in the entertainment room at this point, but he's never been in there. Not even once.

He wants the most basic routine with little repetition because any additional activities would provide far too much choice, and with less to choose from, he can quickly go from doing very little in one place to doing very little in another. It saves a lot of time that can be used waiting for time to pass.

Please head inside when you're ready and proceed to your chosen destination.

While heading towards the corridor, One-ninety-five trips and falls to the floor.

'Oh, for fuck's sake, it was going so well, too!' he bellows.

That's fine. Take a few steps back into the garden, and we'll continue from "Please head inside…".

One-ninety-five gets to his feet and dusts off his knees. 'I'm fine, by the way. Thanks for the concern.'

Don't start. Let's just continue where we left off so we can maintain momentum.

'Momentum,' One-ninety-five scoffs, resetting himself. 'That's all you ever care about.'

Please head inside when you're ready and proceed to your chosen destination.

The walk to the library is tedious. It takes One-ninety-five back through the canteen, up a set of staircases, and around several winding corridors. It's pretty easy to get confused. To be quite honest, there's little reason for so many turns. Whether you take a left or a right, you'll always end up at the library because there are no other rooms in this area for the corridors to lead you to. It's rather pointless if you ask me, although nobody ever does.

The library itself is relatively small—in terms of floor space, that is. The ceiling, however, stands at such a height that you can't even see it when you look up, no matter how much you squint. At the far end of the room, there's a bookcase and ladder so tall they end wherever the ceiling begins, or at least that's what One-ninety-five assumes. He has no real evidence beyond his imagination. He's never climbed particularly high, but he likes to think he's climbed high enough. Whatever that means.

You have two hours to spend in here, One-ninety-five. Lunch will be ready in the canteen once you're done.

One-ninety-five starts climbing the ladder at a cautious pace. He counts every rung that each hand touches, knowing that he usually counts up to fifty before he starts looking at the books. Today, though, he's going for fifty-one.

'Twenty-three?' One-ninety-five says to himself. 'Twenty-four?'

He begins climbing back down the ladder.

What happened now?

'I lost count.'

What? You only have to count up to fifty-one. How difficult is that?

'Difficult enough, clearly.'

Just continue on my mark.

One-ninety-five positions himself near the door and slowly inhales through his nose.

You have two hours to—

'One moment, please!' One-ninety-five snaps.

He inhales through his nose once again, holds it inside his lungs, and exhales gently through his mouth. He repeats this several times and then puts up his thumb.

Oh, you're ready? Have you breathed enough now?

'Don't get funny with me. Just go.'

You have two hours to spend in here, One-ninety-five. Lunch will be ready in the canteen once you're done.

One-ninety-five steps up to the ladder with more purpose and intent than ever and begins to count.

One...

Two...

Three...

And so on—you know how counting works.

This time he reaches fifty-one without skipping a beat. He

starts scanning the selection of books in front of him, books that were previously out of reach, looking for the spine that catches his eye. It's usually the most colourful design or wackiest font that appeals to him most, but this time the most boring spine stands out because it's all the more unique for it being so much plainer than the others.

The book is titled "You Are Here", and that struck a chord with One-ninety-five because he is, in fact, right there, where here is. Here being on the fifty-first rung of a seemingly endless ladder. But then he realises that here can be anywhere, and he's spent too much time either being there or nowhere in an attempt to be here, looking at this very book.

One-ninety-five slides the book from its place, but it slips from his fingers due to its unexpected weight and plummets to the ground.

'For God's sake, who's making these things? Why is that so damn heavy!'

Are you really blaming the book for that? It's a book—just hold on to it. If you're making silly mistakes now, you'll be an absolute mess when we eventually have an audience here.

'You climb this ladder and see how nervous you get.'

I really thought we'd get beyond this part today. It's always the library. Always.

One-ninety-five starts making his way down the ladder, counting down the rungs to stop himself from looking down.

'And he's no help! Why even say that? This isn't part of the scene! Let me reset the book, and until I do, just stop.'

Don't take your frustrations out on me. I'm doing my part just fine.

'That's because you have the easiest bit!'

I beg your pardon. I constantly have to improvise because of your mistakes, and you don't even have any dialogue.

That's exactly what my point was.

'I'm not arguing about this, neither of you two could do better in my position, and you know it.'

ONE-NINETY-FIVE

Stepping off the bottom rung, One-ninety-five picks up the—

'Just be quiet, please. This isn't part of the scene. They don't need to know what I'm doing until I'm back in position with this book on the shelf.'

How will they know what's happening?

'They won't because they don't need to.'

Fine, have it your way.

...SOME MORE TIME GOES BY...

One-ninety-five gets his fingers on either side of the book and slides it from its place. The book is heavier than he expected, but he manages to keep a firm grip on the spine. After all, it's only a book. You'd have to be pretty incompetent to drop it. In fact, you could probably send a chimp to perform the same task, and it would probably do it far more efficiently. It's not like the chimp would need to learn any lines or do anything that requires thought or skill.

'Right, that's it, I'm done.'

Oh, don't be a baby. It's just a joke.

Can you two just stop and get on with the scene?

'Absolutely not. No. That was the last straw. If you think this is so easy, you do it.'

Well, I don't care. Go.

Are you serious? Do you know how important this is?

It's just as important to him as it is to me, and if I have to suffer the loss, that's fine just as long as he does too.

You've got to be kidding me.

'See how childish he is?'

You're both as bad as each other. Just put the book back, and we'll start from the narration. End of discussion.

...BARELY ANY TIME GOES BY...

One-ninety-five carefully removes the book from the shelf and studies it for a moment. The title keeps echoing inside his head, and an urge begins to irritate his skin. He needs to know what's inside the book. He has to open it. Could it be so simple? He had spent so long scanning hundreds of books in preparation for this moment, but he never thought it would take something so plain to inspire him to read again.

And then he realises something:

> The end is the beginning.

* * *

[February 2019]

Before I read this story, my only concern for Warren involved his ability to write and his passion for doing so, but now I was concerned for his mental health. I had seen hints of it before, but I didn't think it was this bad. Not only was he trapped inside his head again, like in *An Ordinary Dream*, but he was also making it a prison for himself.

The protagonist in this story is isolated from whatever world lies beyond the walls. Every day he's going through the same routine to the point where life is on autopilot. No need to think and no use in complaining. That's how it is. I realised this wasn't a fictional character with just a few personality traits of its writer: it was Warren in every way. So was this self-aware parable a cry for help? Was it the only way for him to tell me how he was feeling? There was no other way of looking at it.

Warren goes deep inside his own mind, using three distinct characters to demonstrate how he copes in difficult situations. These characters are preparing to perform in front of a live audience, with each day being a rehearsal. In pursuit of that perfect performance, they neglect entertainment and joy, spending most of their time looking for answers in the library but never climbing higher than the previous day. They simply wait for time to go by so they can try again tomorrow, where I assume One-ninety-five would've become One-ninety-six. But at the end of day one-ninety-five, they finally choose to move on to the next act when they discover a very uninteresting book.

Nothing special sparks this revelation, but I think that's the very point. All it takes sometimes is just another day to change everything—just a random choice with no coincidence or contrived series of events. That's why it ends so abruptly, almost like it's unfinished. Tough times come as sudden as they go. All you need is time. As for the rehearsing, I think it represents how we all train to behave in the real world. We all put up a front to some degree.

The conclusion of this story gave me a little hope because it proved that Warren fantasised about finding his way back. And despite being driven to this prison by his stories, he knew they would also be the catalyst for his escape. Constantly writing was the only way he could find inspiration and reignite his passion, as though he was waiting for that one book on the shelf to catch his eye. And so he accepted that it could take a hundred or more stories to get where he needed to be because, sooner or later, the right story was only one more story away.

MARCH 2019

I used to be pleasantly surprised when Warren uploaded something new. It sometimes just relieved the anticipation, but I always fed off his creativity because it genuinely drove me to do better. And not just for myself but for others, like those I reached through my own writing or talked to at events. I felt I had to do a better job leading by example, and I believe I've managed to do that since I first delved into Warren's work. This is why I owe him this book. I've let him down by not returning what he gave me.

During this month, however, I was no longer anticipating his stories in the same way I used to. It had become a worrying thought, but it wasn't a concern over whether he'd upload again or how long it would take. It was the nature of the next story that caused me unease, and I couldn't help but think it would be the one that finished it all—the story that saw Warren break down and finally call it a day. I wanted so much for him to maintain his level of writing but for it to also manifest itself in a more positive and healthier way.

The next upload provided another look into Warren's head, but this was different; it was the most personal yet troubling insight I ever got into his mind.

Thoughts That Echo

The blinds let in a dusty amber light that struggled to reach the distant corners of the room. He was sat at the table, at the edge of where the light faltered, listening to the rain tapping the window.

The sound of static filled the air.

'You know why we're here, don't you?' a voice said.

'Yes, I do,' he answered.

Nobody spoke for a minute. He turned to the window and gazed at the lights coming from the distant apartment buildings, all shimmering alongside the stars in the sky.

'Do you think you're happy?' the voice said.

'I know I'm happy,' he replied very quickly.

Another minute of silence followed. Vehicles floated by his window, causing the dusty light to glisten and dance with the shadows until the hum of engines faded into rain.

'What's your biggest regret?' the voice continued.

'That's a difficult question. I'd have to think about it a little bit,' he said.

Sirens started in the distance. The sound never rose above the pattering on the window and soon faded into the distance until it was nothing more than a whisper in the wind.

'Do you believe in God?' the voice asked.

'I like to believe I do,' he hesitantly answered.

The oxygen regulation apparatus next to the counter began to whir. It sat above the pressure controller and silicate metering, resulting in a soft vibration that soothed the white noise.

'What is your biggest fear?' the voice went on.

'Ground level,' he replied, his words unsteady.

He picked up the glass of water on the table in front of him and brought it to his lips. The water had a murkiness to it, but one you'd only notice if held up to the light. He put the glass back down without taking a sip.

'Lastly, do you think your thoughts are your own?' the voice said with a firm tone.

'How could I possibly answer that?' he replied.

His attention was drawn to the two cylindrical devices on the table. The design and size of both were very similar, but one had a solid metal casing with a small diaphragm on the side that allowed sound to get in, while the other had a mesh construction that allowed sound to get out. He picked up both devices and waited a couple of minutes, listening to the static that leaked from the mesh of the one device.

Using his thumbs, he rotated one ring to the right, and the other to the left, and the static ceased with a click. He tapped the back of each device with his forefinger, and a small disc was ejected from the top of them. He put the devices down and swapped the discs over, pushing them into invisible slots. Again, he rotated the rings back the other way and the static returned.

'You know why you're here, don't you?' a voice said.

'Yes, I do,' the same voice answered.

'He doesn't know why, but he does know how,' he added.

He attempted to take another sip of water, but he fought the temptation once again, and the glass went down with a clunk.

'Do you think you're happy,' the voice said.

'I know I'm happy,' the same voice quickly replied.

'That's a lie. He couldn't even tell you what happiness meant,' he interjected.

The sound of traffic returned, but this time it was hollow and coming from one of the devices on the table.

'What's your biggest regret?' the voice continued.

'That's a difficult question. I'd have to think about it a little bit,' the same voice said.

'He doesn't have to think about it. He just has to figure out which person he let down the most,' he put in.

He lifted his chin and closed his eyes. Sirens crept out of the device and slowly drifted away.

'Do you believe in God,' the voice asked.

'I like to believe I do,' the same voice hesitantly answered.

'Bullshit. He doesn't believe in anything except the distinction between what is and what isn't, not what might be,' he countered.

The device on the table duplicated the whir of the oxygen regulator, simulating a gentle echo.

'What is your biggest fear?' the voice went on.

'Ground level,' the same voice replied with a tremble.

'The people there. How estranged they all are from one another. It's safer up here.'

He opened his eyes and looked at the glass of water, picturing himself taking a sip.

'Lastly, do you think your thoughts are your own?' the voice said firmly.

'How could I possibly answer that?' the same voice replied.

'They're like waves,' he began, pausing to think. 'They come one after another, and there's no way of knowing how high they will rise or how far they will go, but they all fall back into the same ocean.'

Once again, he picked up the devices, waited, turned the rings, swapped the discs, and reset the rings.

'You know why you're here, don't you?' a voice said.

'Yes, I do,' the same voice answered.

'He doesn't know why, but he does know how,' the same voice added.

'How everything I did led me here and how different life

could've been,' he put in.

There was a clunk from one of the devices, but before he could sort out his thoughts, the voice continued with, 'Do you think you're happy?'

'I know I'm happy,' the same voice replied instantly.

'That's a lie. He couldn't even tell you what happiness meant,' the same voice interjected.

Sirens briefly intruded.

'It's not real, that's why!' he snapped. 'You talk of a state, but it's only felt within a moment. And such a moment is gone just as fast as it came.'

'What's your biggest regret?' the voice quickly continued.

'That's a difficult question. I'd have to think about it a little bit,' the same voice added.

'He doesn't have to think about it. He just has to figure out which person he let down the most,' the same voice put in.

'That's an easy one. Me. I let myself down the most, as selfish as that may seem.'

'Do you believe in God?' the voice asked.

'I like to believe I do,' the same voice hesitantly answered.

'Bullshit. He doesn't believe in anything except the distinction between what is and what isn't, not what might be,' the same voice countered.

The noise from the oxygen regulator was once again duplicated by one of the devices, but this time it had an extra layer and sounded chaotic.

'Because there's no room for doubt. Why waste time on things that exist only in our minds? We spend enough time there as it is.'

'What is your biggest fear?' the voice went on.

'Ground level,' the same voice replied with a tremble.

'The people there. How estranged they all are from one another. It's safer up here,' the same voice said.

'It's lonelier too, but that's the lesser of so many evils,' he put in.

The glass of water was turning a pale white.

'Lastly, do you think your thoughts are your own?' the voice said.

'How could I possibly answer that?' the same voice replied.

'They're like waves,' the same voice began, pausing to think. 'They come one after another, and there's no way of knowing how high they will rise or how far they will go, but they all fall back into the same ocean.'

'They come, and then they go, just like that,' he added. 'The nature of existence. You are here, and then you're not.'

He centred the rings and stood up, turning to the window. He watched the rain, the flickering lights within the cityscape silhouette, and the endless black of the night sky. It was like a painting had come to life. A painting with a dull palette and rotten canvas, unsigned by its painter, yet its design was so elegant and its anonymity so provoking that one could only assume it was by cruel intention.

The horizon was littered with industrial towers that gave warning to an ocean that still glistened under the stars; it was a hopeless battle. No charge would be made in the fight, and whimpering silence would befall nature in its defeat. A pit opened in his stomach as his yearning for sunrise was dampened by the fear of the long shadows it casts. You can only outrun them for so long.

He turned away from the view and said, 'I'm here because I need answers. Answers to why I'm unhappy. I regret not asking the questions sooner, having put my faith into hopes and dreams and expecting life to work out sooner or later. Now I fear it's too late.'

He looked at the glass of water and the pill at the bottom that was almost fully dissolved. 'I'll never know.'

* * *

[March 2019]

This was difficult to get through. I sat and pondered over it for a while after the first reading. I didn't want to believe Warren was feeling this way. I tried to devise an interpretation that would separate him from this story, but only one conclusion made sense.

This dejected character is a projection of Warren's future—where he feels he'll inevitably end up. This is why it's set in a futuristic world, which isn't instantly clear until you realise vehicles are floating across a top-floor apartment window, not to mention all the strange technology it features. He sees himself alone with nobody to talk to, so he forces himself to answer the same questions repeatedly until he finally lets out the truth, which is neatly captured in one paragraph at the end.

This made me wonder if our thoughts being our own was really a question of whether we become what we wanted to be or have just accepted the choices we didn't make. That had to be it. Struggling as an animator, Warren often questioned whether he was always meant to be where he was, and finding a new outlet in storytelling was a temporary reset for him. But the doubts eventually caught up with him and grew through his stories, and that's why he didn't want to share them with the world. He didn't want to be seen as something he didn't believe he was, despite the reassurance right in front of him, so he overlooked the qualities in his stories and let obsession get the best of him.

He clearly knew his mental health was deteriorating, so he revealed his struggle in this story by putting some sort of medication at the bottom of a glass of water that the protagonist is hesitant to drink. I don't want to assume too much because it's a complex topic, but it's hard to see it as anything other than a cry for help, just like One-ninety-five.

As usual, I sent Warren my feedback, leaving out most of the assumptions. I didn't know what else I could do at this point. He needed to talk to someone who could help, not read feedback from me, that's if he was still reading my emails at that point. There was no way of suggesting he should get professional help without offending him, and I couldn't risk having him block me because I'd be shut out from all his work. All I could do was sit back and wait for the next story. Not that I knew if there would be a next one. I just lingered between hope and fear, not knowing where to settle.

APRIL 2019

The next story came as a surprise, not because it was another quick turnaround, but because it was a follow-up to *Relatable Jeff*, one I know he never intended to write. A lot had changed since that first entry, so Warren decided to look back, which people often do when in search of melancholy. I believe he read some of his earlier work and thought revisiting an old story would take him back to a time when things were clear. And so, he gave Jeff a second chance.

Relatable Jeff: Second Chance

Jeff? Are you still there?

Of course you are. You do know I never left, right? I just needed... time. Time to figure out where the plot had gone. I was wrong about it this whole time. I was trying to force a change in your life that you never asked for because I wanted the story to go in a different direction, and I wanted to please the readers and entertain them with an inciting incident. But I see now that I was wrong. The plot was right with you all this time—I just couldn't see it. I'll give you back control, Jeff, and I know how to do it. You don't even have to get up. Everyone deserves a second chance, right? I gave you many chances, but now I'm asking you for just one. Give me that second chance, Jeff.

Jeff stops crying. He's curled up on the floor and doesn't know where he is or what he should do. He's exhausted. With each passing moment, his eyelids get heavier until he can no longer support their weight. Darkness fills his vision, and a sense of weightlessness comes over him as if he were floating in a vacuum far away from the world. It's peaceful, Jeff thinks to himself. Nobody can harm him here. He wants to stay in this place between now and forever, but he knows he can't.

Jeff hears ocean waves in the distance. The sound creeps closer, teasing his ears. Light erupts from the void and pulls him forward, but he's stopped by an arm that doesn't belong to him. He opens his eyes and sees that he'd been an inch away from bashing his face on the back of a dirty bus seat. He looks to his side and sees Judy smirking at him.

'There goes that led foot again,' she says.

The bus driver pokes his head out from his cage. 'Sorry, last time, I promise.'

Jeff removes his earphones and smiles. 'I was having an awful dream. Well, a nightmare.'

'I figured,' Judy replies. 'You were moving—'

Jeff pops in his earphones, resuming the penultimate track of Ocean Waves Volume Ten, readying his demeanour for another day at work. He stares at the window, allowing the world beyond it to become a blur, and time begins to pass like sand through a sieve. It isn't long before his stop comes up, but he isn't paying attention to the journey. Fortunately, Judy is paying attention and reaches across him and presses the stop button. They share a look before she nudges him out of his seat.

They step off the bus and head towards a crossing. Judy comments on the bus driver, but Jeff doesn't hear it because he's still listening to the sound of ocean waves, allowing his brain to be massaged by gentle vibrations. It's the only sound in the world that makes him calm, and that's what he needs to be because his patience is constantly tested at work. So this is his routine, and while it would strike as mundane to most, Jeff is comfortable with it. And that's okay.

They stop at a crossing and wait. Jeff keeps his eyes on the red man while swaying his head in rhythm with the waves in his ears. It was the final track of Ocean Waves Volume Ten, featuring the most gentle waves he's ever heard. If he had a choice to listen to one last sound right before his death, he would choose this one.

The red man disappears, and Jeff steps off the curb with a smile on—oh, a car hits him, and it hits him hard. The driver slams on the brake, and Jeff is thrown forward at speed and lands on the concrete with a sickening thud.

I told you, Jeff. There was a big twist around one of these corners. You just chose the wrong one. You should have stayed on the right path.

Jeff reaches out for his earphones that had landed a few feet away, but life fails to hold on, and everything slowly fades to black.

> Today was the day that Jeff's life changed...
> For the better.

* * *

[April 2019]

As you can see, my initial thoughts were completely wrong. Warren hadn't returned to this story for a sense of clarity or closure. He couldn't find the relief he was after in his earlier stories, so he sought to vent his frustration. He disregarded the purpose of the first part, in which he uses Jeff and the narrator to express two conflicting opinions, and made it about... well, himself. The narrator switched motive to the extreme without good reason, while Jeff was led to slaughter for the sake of it.

Jeff's death was Warren telling me that he was done. He didn't want to wait for the next story to see if things would change. This became the last one he wrote—or at least the last he ever shared with me. And it was a sad one.

NOVEMBER 2020

So, we've come full circle. It's been a challenging project, both technically and mentally. It feels strange looking back. I can't believe I started writing this in early 2019. The world has drastically changed since then, which is partly why it's taken so long to get to this stage of the book, along with the fact that I really miss Warren's stories. I relied on them too much to keep me going.

It's now been nineteen months since his last upload. I often check *rename later*, but it's been dormant ever since he killed Jeff. I haven't stopped trying to contact him, especially given the pandemic the world is suffering through as I write this, but after going so long without receiving a reply or an upload, I'm mainly sending him emails out of habit. I only want to encourage him to write again and help push his work into the public eye; I know he can be successful if he gets his mind right. Putting that aside, I just want him to be okay.

I'm sorry I can't give you the ending I was hoping for. I might wait a couple of months before I consider this finished. Maybe he'll reply. Maybe he's better now. I hope he reads this book and sees how much his stories mean to me and how much they could mean to others if he gave them a chance. If that's not enough, I don't know what is.

FEBRUARY 2021

Back in October 2019, I sent Warren an early draft of this book and hoped he would read it and give the approval I wanted from him. I recently sent another draft to him, trying to find some closure for a proper ending, and he finally replied.

I haven't opened the email yet. I'm really nervous but excited at the same time. I just wanted to get my thoughts down on the page beforehand. I've been waiting for this for a long time now. I might not even keep this part in—I'm just rambling to give you a sense of where my mind is at. I'm hoping Warren has been inspired by what I've been doing because I'll have finally given back to him. It's what he deserves. It's what this story deserves, too. But anyway, that's enough stalling. Right, the email.

Dear JD,

I started writing because I had ideas and concepts that could be explored in short stories. From there, I progressed into more complex themes, as any writer naturally does, and I spent more time with these ideas than I had first planned. It made me tired. Really tired. I wasn't functioning the same way, and it wasn't healthy. Eventually, I gave up. I just didn't want to do it anymore. I couldn't even if I tried. But it wasn't because I was obsessed with questions of identity and purpose. It wasn't because I became depressed or mentally ill. It wasn't even due to any fear of criticism or failure.

    It was because of you.
    Just you.
    It always was.

You've been trying to figure me out for a long time now, like I'm the riddle in your life that you need to solve before you can move on, so you imprinted your ideas within my work and made me out as some flawed, desperate character in need of your help. And through all that, you convinced yourself you'd feel accomplished if I gained success with your guidance. You pushed, and you pushed, and you pushed. What made you think I was looking for a mentor? I only started sharing my stories because I thought you'd simply read them and move on like any normal person should. I did expect some analysis, but not a psychological one.

    And then there's the advice: *think about your audience; cater to a crowd; adjust for the readers because they won't adjust for you; write something longer, but not too long; you should get an editor and try to get published; develop an online presence and build a brand of yourself.*

Countless emails. Do you think I wanted any of this? Or just needed it? When was it up to you to decide what was best for me? You twisted everything. I wrote stories that relayed back to our conversations because I thought you would eventually understand what I wanted, but you kept seeing it as a cry for help.

I should've known what I was in for when you first read *The Perfect Twist*. You suggested I make it clearer for the readers even though it was designed to trip them up. I wanted it to be tricky, but despite me telling you this, you still added numbers to the story to make it easier for yourself. The whole idea of the story was for readers to pay attention to the perspective shifts and not rely on any guidance. You have to learn to accept that not everything can be how you want it to be, just like I accept that people might not like a confusing narrative.

Then you read *A Tale of Two Pronouns* and understood it to be about a lack of communication. It wasn't too far off, but you were looking at it the wrong way. It was about misinterpretation. Seeing something as it isn't and letting it ruin what is. Sound familiar? I wasn't bothered by your comments on this story, but there was a trend forming that I wish I had been more wary of at the time.

Relatable Jeff was next, and you actually recognised that you might be getting pushy, but you picked apart the story so much that you missed the entire point of it. How did you conclude it was, in part, a criticism of romantic fiction? Is it too inconceivable that someone simply doesn't enjoy a genre? Or do they need a deep resentment to justify a preference? Jeff was the average person from your point of view, not mine. To me, he was just someone forced into a moment that could change his life but decided to go against that change. The narrator refuses to see that Jeff never wanted or asked for it. Can you see the parallels now? Jeff was happy with his life, but the narrator only saw what he wanted to see.

I quickly moved on from that story and tried to forget about your "analysis". I focused on *The Unexamined Life* and *Zoia*, making sure they were independent of the problems you were causing. And against my better judgement, I let you read them. That was my mistake. Your response was fine at first, but behind your emails, you plotted to make me "think like an author". Could you have first asked if I wanted to be one? Or at least one that fits your description? What even is an author to you? Someone that moulds their image and stories to appease a crowd? Is it success and money?

I started to struggle with ideas because I was stuck inside my head with doubts and worries growing by the day. I decided to externalise that struggle and crafted a story called *An Ordinary Dream*. Some elements were taken from my actual dreams to give it a sense of the surreal, but the story was essentially me living with all the negative thoughts growing in my head, taking up so much space that it simply couldn't be contained. So, you were pretty spot on with this one. But one vital detail was left out: you planted the seed that allowed that tree to grow. And grow it did.

Then I found out you betrayed my trust. You went around showing my story without my permission, and you proudly presented me with the results. I honestly couldn't believe it. I had to pretend I didn't read that email because it made me anxious to think how many of my stories you were editing and presenting to people. Why would you even think of doing that to me? You must have known how I'd feel about it, or you wouldn't have done it in secret.

I wanted to shut you out for good, but I couldn't stop myself from uploading the second part of *The Unexamined Life*. It was like an unhealthy habit I couldn't shake. And, as expected, I got your typical type of feedback in return. You always started with a fair discussion about what each part meant, which I was never bothered by, but then it had to reveal something about me. It had to define my personality and motivation. You couldn't stop yourself.

I wanted to tell you that I didn't need your help, but I tried doing it in my own way because I'm not as confident as you make me out to be in your book. Yes, I can stand up in front of a crowd in one isolated moment, but that doesn't mean I was ever comfortable doing so. I was at that festival because I wanted to try something new while pushing myself to meet like-minded people. It's not something I do very often because I don't find it easy to talk to people I don't know, and even when I do, I don't speak my full mind. I just don't—or didn't—have that ability. So I tried using my stories.

I thought *[APPLAUSE]* would help you see what you were doing—putting me on a stage where I didn't want to be, not letting me get a word in. But you managed to convince yourself that I had issues with an audience and their judgement. That's not even close. I don't mind people giving honest feedback, good or bad, but I do mind when you force me into a spotlight before I'm even ready. You even manipulated our conversations to keep up the lie. You just excuse yourself with:

"I can't remember the whole conversation because it was a long time ago."

So much of what we talked about was left out, but I don't even know if you're aware of what you're doing.

Shortly after, I rushed up *Silhouettes and Epithets*, hoping it would help you finally understand that what you falsely saw in me were simply the things you were missing. If you hadn't refused to look at yourself in the mirror, you would've seen that you're the one scared to put your work out there because you fear failure, not me. You don't want to write for a magazine, and this book proves it. You did this because you wanted to write for yourself but were too critical to finish a story, so you relied on my work instead.

I tried to find some normality by going back to *The Unexamined Life*, but you read *Part III* and theorised that I was looking for a conclusive answer to whether my stories are my own; you desperately wanted there to be some profound meaning behind my work. And then you suggested that writing for myself as a hobby was a bad thing. Why would that be the case? This really got to me, and I became determined to show you your real self.

You took a while to read *A Day in the Life of a Serial Killer*, you were too busy indulging in yourself, but as soon as you sent the feedback, I knew what was coming. I knew exactly how you'd misunderstand it. The paranoid neighbour wasn't my interpretation of your interpretation of me—it was just you. Because, just like him, you create radical scenarios in your head and convince yourself something is an objective truth when it's entirely made up. You've unwittingly become the unreliable narrator in your own personal fiction.

I gave up trying to put you in front of a mirror and went back to writing the stories I enjoyed reading. I started with *The Reaper's Commission,* an idea I'd been looking forward to working on, but I was miserable writing it because I was too aware of what you would say—what twist you would put on it. But out of all the nonsense you came up with, you got one thing right: I was stuck staring at a blank sheet of paper, unwilling to dirty its surface, just like Adam. That's how meaningless I think my writing is now.

I went back to finish *The Unexamined Life,* and you concluded that Jimmy finally took back control. But, like you said: "not everything is as it seems." Jimmy was always in control; he was destined to make the same mistake over and over again, just like I was by uploading story after story, hoping you would see the truth or simply find entertainment and nothing more. As you might guess, I never used my intended ending for *The Unexamined Life,* and I have you to blame for that.

I was really struggling with ideas at this point. I didn't want to send you any more stories, but every time I finished one, I couldn't help it. I didn't know how to cut you off. It was like I had to see it through to overcome it. Like it was the only way I could get back to how writing made me feel before I met you.

I eventually came up with *A Tale Untold*. This story was designed to have multiple meanings, depending on the reader; all interpretations are unique and personal. I gave up trying to create one linear path because I knew you'd come up with your own meaning regardless of what I did. But to me, this story is about all those other stories I would never write because I was somewhere else at the time. Mentally, that is. What this story meant to you was yet another reflection of me because you wouldn't let me be separate from it. It couldn't be personal to you because you're wilfully ignorant of your struggles.

One-ninety-five was only the second story you almost got right, but only because this story fully embraced how I felt and fit your narrative perfectly. It was just too easy for you. The only thing you got wrong was the reason I was locked in that mental prison, but because getting it right would implicate yourself, you turned to your own fiction.

And then we get to *Thoughts That Echo*. This was the last attempt at trying to get you to see reality. You were the sole inspiration for this story, which is what you always wanted. Whatever you concluded in your feedback wasn't a concern of mine anymore. After I uploaded this story, I didn't want to continue writing. When you're done with this email, go back and read this story again. Read it carefully.

That really was going to be the last. I was so tired of thinking about it. All I ever wanted was to take the ideas out of my head and mould them into stories, but now my head is filled with anxiety and doubts that you put there. But I still went back to *Relatable Jeff*. I felt it had to be concluded so I could put writing to rest alongside Jeff. That's all there was to it.

I hope you now understand how difficult it was for me to write this email. I've wanted to send it for months, mentally drafting it in my head, but I finally forced myself to start typing, and it got easier with every word. I didn't plan on being this harsh. I didn't want to bring you down because it's not the kind of person I am. Not usually. But I realised you need to hear this no matter how cruel I come across. It's better for both of us this way.

So, there's your ending, all neatly wrapped up. You can have my stories and publish this book of yours, even though you probably would have anyway. I hope it brings you what you're looking for. But stop contacting me. I'm tired, and I've moved on.

All I ever wanted was to tell stories, not for you or anyone else, but for myself.

But you polluted it.

You are the reason I stopped writing.

DEAR JD,

I've already given you enough, but I'll leave you with this final reveal:

> **Sometimes** it's difficult to find the right words.
> **You** can ponder for days and still not ease the struggle.
> **Only** one way forward: let the words guide themselves.
> **See** where they take you and hope to find meaning among them.
> **What** at first looks like chaos can often conceal peace.
> **You** simply have to look closer, beyond intent.
> **Want** and need should not always produce the same outcome.
> **To** find meaning is to find yourself—if you find it well.
> **See** everything clearly by unwinding the chaos, and then you'll know peace.

* * *

[February 2021]

It's all my fault. He's right. My obsession destroyed his passion. I don't know what else to say except... I'm sorry. I'm tempted to go back and change this book or just delete it altogether, but I can't. I'm still obsessed. I need this. I need people to see me. I want praise and validation, and I can't help it. I want what others have, but I don't even know what I'm missing to understand what I need. Does everyone else even know what they have?

I looked back at *Thoughts That Echo*, and I see it now. The character wasn't Warren: it was me. He was helping me answer all the questions I was too afraid to ask myself. Yet, for all the answers I have now, I don't know the answer to the most important question.

Are your thoughts your own?

I thought I knew, but I got it so wrong. And Warren put it plain and simple: I'll never know. That's the pill I have to swallow. I have to be okay with not knowing things because not everything has to have a deeper meaning—is that it? Isn't that searching for meaning itself? What's the point of it all, then?

I'm searching for meaning because it brings purpose, and that's more than just being here. I don't want to just be here because one day I won't be, and then what was it all for? I want a destiny, and I don't know why. It's like a sickness. It's too easy to blame the world and the people in it because they've created these barriers and expect you to climb them alone and... I'm doing it again—refusing to take responsibility. I took someone's passion from them to serve my own ego. I'm my own problem, and I don't know how to get away from myself. How can I fix it?

I need to think for a moment.

HERE

The worst part about all of this is that I'm still going to release this book. In all honesty, I don't know if it's worse if I do or don't publish it. Wouldn't it be cruel if everything I did to him was for nothing? Or maybe it would give him peace if I scrap it all now and pretend we never met. But I don't want that. I need this out in the world so he knows that I'm sorry and that I'll be different from now on. This journey has changed me for the better. It has, hasn't it? What's the point of all of this otherwise? I know I've been an awful and selfish friend, but I need to know what to do next. Help me. This feels like the middle of a story, not the end. There should be redemption and personal growth, and... resolution.

I never once considered that maybe he just liked telling stories. It was like an escape, but I put up walls that kept him contained. So, I need him to see this. I need him to know that I'm sorry so I can move on. I need a satisfying conclusion. The audience needs it, too. Don't you?

What am I doing? It's like I haven't learned anything at all. I need to stop trying to be something or somewhere I'm not. I need to stop altogether.

But where do I go without Warren's stories to guide me?

I made them so important to me. Too important.

What do I do now? I can't go back to how it was before Warren.

I think I need to stop thinking for a while.

This probably isn't the ending you wanted.

It's definitely not what I wanted.

I'm going to stop trying to be what I'm not and be myself for a while.

That's it, isn't it? I got it backwards this whole time.

I need to just be here before I can get there. Wherever there might be.

I want to be here—I have to.

I don't have any other choice.

>I am here...
>and now so are you.

Acknowledgements

It's taken me almost five years to finish this book, and I couldn't have done it without having the right people around me.

Connor, Maccy, and Mike, you've all kept me sane through the years, and I can't imagine where I'd be without you all.

Jane, you were the first to read this book, and I can't put into words how grateful I am for everything. Your kindness never goes unnoticed.

Mum and Dad, all this was made possible because of you.

Reader, whoever you are, thank you for reading—unless you skipped to the end, in which case, thank you for giving it a shot.